TRIANGULATION: BENEATH THE SURFACE

THE 2016 EDITION OF PARSEC INK'S ANNUAL CONFLUENCE OF SPECULATIVE FICTION ANTHOLOGY

Published by Parsec Ink, a subsidiary of Parsec, Inc.

ISBN-10: 0-9828606-8-4
ISBN-13: 978-0-9828606-8-7

Cover Art: Benjamin Hitmar
Cover Design: Paul Stefko
Editor: Jamie Lackey
Assistant Editors: Kathryn Board, Douglas Gwilym, Frank Oreto, Laine Wooliscroft, and Jon Carroll Thomas.

Parsec Ink is a subsidiary of Parsec, a non-profit literary organization based in Pittsburgh, PA. For more information, visit our website at: parsec-sff.org

Parsec Ink
PO Box 3681
Pittsburgh, PA 15230-3681

CONTENTS

How to Build a Better Mermaid

Mary J. Daley

My grandmother stood barefoot in the sand, near her grey-shingled house, and watched me approach. Her eyes were barely visible under puckers of sun-weathered skin.

I turned to my father. "I don't want to stay."

"It's only for the summer." He placed my suitcase down on the worn boardwalk, kissed the top of my head, turned and walked back through the dunes to the gravel parking lot where our taxi would return him to the airport.

I knew nothing about the person he just left me with. My mother had never mentioned any of this. Not the east coast, not the ocean, not her mother. It was my dad who sprung this on me after he landed a part in a television pilot that was to shoot in Vancouver, and although he wished his big break hadn't followed so soon after mom's death, he thought it was a positive serendipity of sorts receiving this invite from my grandmother.

But as far as I was concerned, if my grandmother was the sort of person I should spend time with, then how come Mom had never, ever mentioned her?

When I turned back to the house, with the wind rattling its screen door and sand covering the front steps, my grandmother went back inside, without an invitation to follow her. I found her in the kitchen kneading dough. Her hands were purple with protruding veins and her knuckles leaned like listeners towards her thumbs.

"Your mother teach you how to make bread?" she asked.

I shook my head.

"What did she teach you?"

"Lots of things."

"Anything useful? Anything to help you make your way in this world?"

I wasn't sure what she meant by that. Mom never stopped teaching me things. Even when she was sick, she taught me how to do a handstand, to walk three whole steps on my palms, to apply lipstick, whistle with four fingers, and to finally achieve a full-pointe position. But I wasn't sure if any of this would help me make my way in this world.

"Do you want to learn how to make bread?"

I nodded and my grandmother ushered me closer.

My grandmother wasn't anything like my mother. Not by a mile. But that summer she taught me things that she said she once taught my mother. Like how to debone a fish, mend a net, and shuck an oyster. Better yet, she helped me to accept them as a food choice, and not just for the one time experience of sliding a perfectly contained morsel of sea down my throat.

And finally, after I had been with her a month, she led me down to the beach under a full and yellow moon and taught me magic.

I laughed when she first used the word magic. It was more of a nervous laugh because by this point I knew my grandmother was not one to joke. We hadn't eaten that day because she said we had to feel hungry for the magic to work.

"Go to the tideline, where the darker sand marks the ocean's last reach, and with your back to the water take seven steps forward." She gave me a gentle shove in the direction of the water as if I couldn't have found it on my own.

I did what she instructed, wondering at first if this was some sort of game where I was suppose to ask, *Mother may I.* After I took the required steps, she came over, knelt, and traced a circle in the sand around me.

"What sea creature would you like to see return to the ocean from this very spot?" she asked.

I laughed again. She looked up at me. Her floral dress gaped at the neckline to reveal wrinkled cleavage. Her brown cardigan billowed hunchback across her shoulders, and her grey curls looked rather feral in the wind. She expected an answer.

I shrugged. "Maybe a mermaid?"

She sighed and sat back on her bare heels. "A bit fantastical, wouldn't you say?"

Feeling stupid, I sputtered, "A walrus then?"

"You meant what you first said, and what you first said is all that the magic will now listen to." She began to trace the form of a mermaid, telling me to step aside so she could do it justice. When she finished she went back to the house and gathered a blue plastic tarp, two buckets, and a steak knife. She spread out the tarp near the ungainly sketch of the mermaid.

"Scoop out the first few inches of sand within the lines, and place them on top of this tarp so it doesn't mix much with the other sand on the beach."

I nodded and went to work. When I finished, she handed me a bucket. "Now fill this with what you find along the tideline. Live things are best."

I followed her, watching her fill her bucket with bits of driftwood, a dead fish, seaweed, three sun-browned jellyfish, clams, and bits of bone. She let out a small cackle when she found a glistening, white seagull with half its body buried in the sand. I grimaced when she picked up the carcass and set it in her pail. I slowly filled my own pail with mostly broken shells.

When our buckets were full, we went back to her sketch. We spilled our bounty within the lines. The stars shone down on our treasure.

Then my grandmother produced a live crab from her cardigan pocket and began to pull off each of its legs.

I no longer found anything fun about this game. "Is it okay if I go inside? I don't really need a mermaid," I said.

"Hush. Don't be a baby."

"But why are you doing that to it?"

"It will ruin the magic if it crawls back over the line." She placed the live crab with its amputated appendages in the middle of our pile. My stomach was now making audible noises from hunger and uneasiness. My mother would never have done something like this. She was the type to carry spiders out of our apartment in Kleenex, letting them loose in the corridor.

Grandmother then picked up the knife, came over and stood in front of me. She grabbed both of my tight brown braids in one hand and without my consent cut them off, leaving the remainder of my hair crooked, short and freed. She then grabbed one of my sunburnt arms by the elbow and stripped off a long, delicate white piece of my flesh that was already peeling. It was over before I even had a chance to pull back my arm.

I clenched my fists at my sides as I fought away tears, and watched in silence as she placed the pieces of me inside the drawing. She then pulled her pipe from her sweater's other pocket.

"That's all there is to it," she said, as she lit the pipe. "Now cover it over with the sand from the tarp and wet that sand with seawater. Use the buckets. When you're done come back to the house and I'll fix you something to eat." With that she left me alone on the beach.

I looked down at my two braids. One lay near the crab. The other lay across the wing of the dead seagull. Both braids were still intact, held somewhat in their crisscross formations by their green hair elastics. My mother had liked my long hair.

First thing tomorrow I was calling my dad to come and fetch me. I now fully understood why my mother had never mentioned my grandmother. She was bat-shit crazy.

Regardless, I was compelled to follow her instructions because I half-wanted to believe in all this nonsense.

When I came into the kitchen a while later, she was sitting at the table under the light of a bare bulb. "We still have a few hours of waiting before the ocean covers her. Would you like some pie?'

I nodded. My head felt much lighter without my braids.

———————————

When we went back down to the beach the moon was directly above us and the last wave was at the very edge of our sand-covered pile.

We stood and watched as each new wave moved across it.

"The first wave over will join all our gathered material," Grandmother whispered. "The second will divide it into flesh and fin. The third to the seventh wave will build its strength."

We watched. Nothing changed at first but after the fifth wave there was a noticeable shift. When the wave retreated a sand-coated limb reached out. I stepped behind my grandmother and closed my eyes.

She grabbed my arm and yanked me forward again. "Don't ever shy from what you have caused," she said.

By now, a young girl was awkwardly turning onto her stomach. She had my color hair and my freckles, but half way down her sandy body, greyish-blue scales glittered. My thoughts went immediately to the city's huge market and all those lines of red snapper and salmon with their silvery, slippery bodies laid out on ice. I shivered when she turned her head and looked at me. Her brown eyes matched the color of the crab's shell. She looked terrified.

She struggled to move forward. Her limbs were weak and foreign to her. Her tail still half buried in sand.

"Should we help her?" I asked.

"No, she doesn't have the mindset to know you're helping and may bite. It's a nasty bite, too, these creations can give. Don't worry. The tide will soon free her."

Sure enough, with each new wave creating depth, her tail began to move back and forth like a moored boat. She seemed reluctant to leave her spot though, gripping the beach sand with her hands. Eventually, she let go and began to swim away. She soon disappeared beneath the dark water.

"And that's that. The ocean gained another creature." Grandmother pulled her sweater tight around herself.

"Will she come back?'

My grandmother shrugged. "It's difficult to predict such things. And if she does, it's difficult to predict what her disposition might be. This means you must be careful when you swim. Don't go too far out and keep vigilant. But the truth is, she'll probably be long gone by morning. It is a big ocean out there."

I stared out at the dark water and its relentless waves. "Why do you do this, Grandmother?"

She shrugged. "Because once upon a time it was a useful tool."

The next morning I came down to the kitchen just as my grandmother was pulling a tray of warm biscuits from the oven.

"Did your mother have much pain? In the end?" she asked, as she placed them on the table.

I nodded. "Some."

"And never once did she ask for me?"

I shook my head.

She looked down at her hands. I looked at the biscuits and was just about to ask for one when she cleared her voice and said, "Your father should have sent word earlier that she was sick. She, herself, should have had the good sense to come home. This place has always been good to us, at least to the women folk. I can't remember my mother or grandmother ever having a single sick day."

"They lived here too?"

She nodded. "And those before them. Here on this shore if not in this house."

"Did they know how to make things too? Like sea things?" I asked.

She started to untie the knot in her apron but thought better of it and rubbed at her hands instead. "Each generation taught the next. How it started, who knows? My own mother was best at making cod, but she made a mermaid once, which is how I knew I could probably make one, too, when you asked. She sent hers off to search for my father, whose fishing vessel disappeared out past the bay a day prior. She gave the creature one of her eyes so it would recognize him. But it was all for naught, for the creature never returned and neither did my father. Maybe not all for naught, for her eye patch always reminded me not to take magic too seriously or I'd end up regretting it."

I reached up and touched the ends of my hair and was suddenly very thankful that my grandmother didn't take magic as seriously as her mother had. "Did my mother know magic?"

"Your mother wanted nothing to do with it." Her voice suddenly gained another level. "I could have taught her how to create enough fish to fill a dozen nets, but she shunned this useful gift for a pair of dance slippers and weekly classes from a woman a mild breeze could have carried across town. And for the life of me, I could not convince her of the impracticability of it. We had a falling out and she left for Toronto when she was barely eighteen. And then she up and marries an actor and calls me the unrealistic one." She sighed then. "So, did she become any good at it?"

"Dancing?"

"No, hair pulling, pay attention. Yes, did she become any good at dancing?"

"Yes, but it was too difficult for her to juggle work, dance and me, so she gave up dance. "

"See. I was right. I knew I was right. But she wouldn't listen to sense." Grandmother stared out the window then, forgetting about me. I took a biscuit and left her to her thoughts.

On the evening before my father came to reclaim me, I went down to the shore to skip rocks. My mother had taught me this, not my grandmother. I wasn't sure I wanted to go back. I liked the ocean, but I missed my father.

"Are you out there?" I yelled at the water. "I really wanted to see you again. Hopefully, I'll come back next summer."

I knew this was wishful thinking. I had been looking out for the young mermaid since we created her, but she never returned. I was beginning to think I had dreamt the whole thing up.

I scanned the white caps for a while longer anyway.

When my father took my suitcase from me the next day and hurried me down the boardwalk towards the car, talking non-stop of a possible new start in Vancouver, my grandmother stood there with her arms crossed and one eyebrow raised. I was still unsure of who or what she was. I looked over my shoulder at her, smiling, hoping it looked like a thank you. She was a far harsher creature than my gentle mother, but I decided I liked her anyway. I was even beginning to understand the division that had separated them. One was blessed with grace and the other with grit. Like sea and sand.

We never went to Vancouver. Dad's pilot wasn't picked up. Instead, he went back to tending bar most evenings, leaving me more and more alone.

He remarried when I was fifteen. I was blessed with a brother and frequent requests that I try to get along with my new mother. I wasn't able to comply and my father and I began to drift apart.

High school was torture. I finished with low marks and enough slander across my Facebook wall to strip away any magic I thought I knew.

I missed my mother terribly during those years, although, the missing went from one substantial piece to a million smaller ones. I missed my grandmother, too, but circumstances never brought me back to her. She had tried to remain in contact with me, but I never returned her letters. She even sent me money for airfare once. I used the money for a tattoo. If it was any consolation, it was of a mermaid.

When I turned twenty-one, I received a letter from my grandmother's lawyer. She had died and left me her house on the ocean. It was a difficult gift to accept after shunning her attempts at contacting me. But I was alone and drifting, and I wanted nothing more than to belong somewhere. Anywhere. And here was my grandmother asking me to become the next woman of that house. I could have come up with a hundred worse places to end up.

I arrived on a July evening and I took my time walking the worn boards, taking in the sharp blades of sea grass and perfect domes of sand. I used the key that was given to me and stepped into the foyer where the trapped smell of warm, salted wood reminded me of something Grandmother had once told me. That magic isn't all spells and trickery. It is organic and transferrable. It can come and go like sandpipers and plovers, and that it's neither inherently good nor bad. It's simply about finding the ability to make something new from something else, and that absolutely everything had this ability.

I took my time exploring, still slightly conflicted, only because my mother never wished it for herself and never wished this for me.

Flowerpots, half full of soil, sat on most of the windowsills. The flour bin still held flour. My grandmother's bedroom was bare of blankets. A comb sat at the side of the small enamel sink in the bathroom. It held some of her grey hair. In the second bedroom, where I had slept that first summer, lured to sleep every night by the waves, was the same narrow bed. I stretched out on it and was soon asleep and dreaming about a group of women mending nets, while one woman did pirouettes behind them.

It was difficult getting used to having this much space. Even on cloudy days the sky seemed too much. Most days, I felt the ocean deserved much better than my unenthusiastic gaze.

I had never forgotten the mermaid that I had made with my grandmother, but I had long given up hope on seeing her again. So, I was shocked and delighted when she appeared in the surf one morning not far from my front door. I had lived here a little over three months at the time and was almost sealed in my solitude. But seeing her shook me free from myself and I left the stoop still holding my coffee, hurrying towards her through the soft, wet sand. She raised herself up and hissed a warning. I stopped. She had grown as I had, but was very thin and muscular. Survival must have equated to speed in her world. From the scars that lacerated her neck and arms it appeared that she wasn't always successful avoiding harm. Her hair was long and knotted, and held bits of net and shell and even plastic. But it was her eyes that made me swallow and glance away from her. She was angry. Perhaps it was because Grandmother and I left her to navigate this world of hers on her own like my mother had once left me to navigate mine.

But I was the far crueler one for I hadn't provided this mermaid with a single memory of a mother. She had a right to her anger. My grandmother's words came back to me then. Don't close your eyes to what you have caused.

I trudged back to the house and visited each room. I found my great grandmother's eye patch. I found my grandmother's arthritis creams she once spread over her knuckles, and I found, jutting out slightly between her mattress and her box spring, a journal. My mother's name was on the inside cover. The pages were worn with reading. I brought it up to my nose and smelled my grandmother's hand cream on its pages. I slid to the floor and I read. I read until the darkening dusk made it impossible. My mother was seventeen in her journal and wrote about ballet and travel and escaping and fame and about Grandmother's failure to understand. My mother's words were full of life and I filled up on them the same way my grandmother must have had night after night, after she applied her cream. I wondered if my grandmother ever came to the conclusion that what was useful was an individual measure.

I got up and looked out the window. The sky now housed a full moon so I hurried from room to room gathering more of these women's lives. I went down onto the beach to the edge of the tide and I took seven giant steps inland. Mother may I.

Here I sketched a mermaid and filled her with all the small pieces of the women of this household, along with driftwood and oysters and a pair of tattered pointe slippers with their dirty pink laces. I thought how difficult it must have been for my gruff, pipe smoking, magic-making grandmother to have once carted her young daughter to all those after school ballet and hip hop lessons. How difficult it was to lose her to a desire she could make little sense of.

The last thing I placed on the heap was my mother's journal, and then I covered it all in sand and I waited. I waited for the incoming waves to work their magic. Soon, a woman appeared so like my mother that I reached out boldly and slid a hand down the scales of her tail. She looked long and empty at me but this was okay for I hadn't made her for me. I sat and waited for the tide to take her out to sea and towards her own daughter.

And as I sat there under that huge moon, I hoped that they would find and learn from each other. The daughter could show her mom how to avoid fishing nets, low tides and sharks, and the mother could tell her daughter how incredibly proud she was of her for learning to maneuver these rough seas on her own.

Mary J. Daley currently resides on a small farm in Ontario, Canada , where she spends a great deal of time trying to get her chestnut mare to like her. Her publishing credits include Electric Spec, Fantastique Unfettered, Lore *and others.*

THE JESSAMINE GARDEN

JOHN LINWOOD GRANT

I have been to see Julian St Claire again.

The doctor was horrified, but he provided me with more ointments and emollients, employing bandages soaked in liquid paraffin to cover the worst of the pustules. An injection steadied my pulse, and stopped the trembling down my left side. The fever will abate on its own. It usually does.

I gave him an additional ten dollars, and made such promises as seemed appropriate. I knew that I would not keep them.

My sister watches as I write this entry in my journal. It is more difficult to form letters with the linen wrapped around each finger, but I have devised a method of wedging the pen in place. I notice that my writing has deteriorated, an irregularity of stroke which matches the stagger of my heartbeat. It does not matter, for the words are still legible and they will serve. They will be the only record of the time I spent in the Jessamine Garden....

I do not think we met by chance on that slow Virginia morning. I will not name the exact area, for I will be jealous until the end, and I know that my sister will never speak of the place. That I should drive the buggy up the wrong road, distracted by my thoughts, that I should draw up so close to that decayed colonial home... it was meant to be. As I had long been forgotten by the God of my childhood, perhaps the mercurial Fate of the Greeks and Romans had willed it. The capricious Fortuna, her blind eyes smiling on a faithless man.

The house itself was not unusual, a smaller version of the great plantation houses further south. A man of about thirty years stood by the portico, the columns wreathed in vines unknown to me, thick tendrils grasping at old plaster. He was slim, much my own height but not especially well-favoured in feature. His eyes were too large, his jaw too narrow, for him to be called handsome. I reined in my horse, and called out if he knew a better road that I could take to continue my journey.

"Come down, sir." He smiled and beckoned. "Take a julep with me, and I shall set you right."

I was thirsty enough, and the mare was flagging. He pointed to a stone trough by a barn.

"Let her rest awhile, too."

I returned his smile, and eased myself down from the buggy. Polio had weakened my left leg, and a bullet in Mexico had shattered the hip above it. I was a poor pedestrian, as he could see. I took up my stick, and was gratified that he removed his cream linen jacket and assisted me in watering the horse. We introduced ourselves as we did so, and he led the way around the side of the house.

A walled garden lay at the rear, ancient brick of a reddish hue, and we entered something which might have graced an English country house. On first glance it was a little overdone, perhaps, but not extraordinary in any way.

"My garden," said Julian St Claire. He nodded to a stone bench not far away. "We might sit out here, perhaps, Mr. Crane?"

Windows in the full-length French style opened into the gloomy interior of his home, but the garden itself was bathed in sunlight. I was grateful to rest as he fetched refreshments. After a few moments he brought out a tray holding two large glasses and a large Venetian jug.

I took my glass eagerly, thanking him, and sipped the coolness of what I had assumed would be a mint julep. The bourbon was there, but mint had never graced this liquid. There was a bitterness, not unpleasant but unexpected. He sat down beside me, wished me good health as he drank.

"Local herbs," he said, his gaze darting to the garden. "An acquired taste, perhaps."

I assured him that it was most refreshing, and looked around. Yellow-flowered jessamine scrambled along and over the brick walls, its perfume on the warm air, its long stems insinuating it into neighbouring bushes and trees at every opportunity. Beneath it lay thickly planted beds which covered the space of half an acre, interspersed with neat gravel paths. No soil could be seen between the plants, which merged and tangled with each other wherever I looked. But I could see that it was managed, not left to grow wild. There were tender plants there which would have been overwhelmed by hardier ruffians without a hand to guide them.

"The walls," I said, "I presume they keep the winter cold out?"

"Somewhat." He nodded. "I have my ways, as well. Bell jars and cold-frames, cloches and manure beds, even an ice-house to keep some tubers and bulbs dormant until the right time."

He leaned closer to me, and I caught the same bitter scent from him as from the drink, though I could not place it. My head was light from the bourbon, and I laughed, not knowing why.

"Do you have many visitors, seeking the secrets of your art?"

"I do not advertise, sir." He shook his head. "I fear that many would come to harm here if I did."

I could not grasp his meaning. "How so?"

"Come." He waited as I employed my stick, and took me down the main path which bisected the garden. As he named his plants, he stroked them, caressing stems and leaves as a man might do to his hound.

"Rue, whose touch causes great welts to appear upon the skin, especially in bright light..."

I looked at the intricate grey-green foliage, the noon-day sun strong upon the leaves, but said nothing.

"The greater celandine, which brings rashes and eruptions, as does this arum low down, see, with its strange saponins and other chemicals. Monkshood..." He tore off a feathery leaf and chewed on it. "A brutal poison when consumed—the tingling and burning presage eventual failure of the heart and nervous system—"

"Sir, Mr. St Claire," I said, but he raised his hand to quell my obvious alarm.

"I am as one with this place. I grew up here, absorbed the riches of my garden and came to understand them. I catch the nuance in each leaf, catalogue and admire it." He brushed the stand of monkshood with affection. "Step closer, sir."

I limped to his side.

"Now hold out your hand."

It is difficult to say why I did what he asked. The bourbon, the heady scent of the garden? As I lifted my free hand, one of his fingertips touched mine, and I gasped as a burning sensation ran up that digit. Lifting it to see what had occurred, I saw a reddened patch the size of a penny coin on my skin.

"It will pass in minutes," he reassured me.

I did not, at the time, understand the significance of this moment. Awkward, I agreed to one last sip of his drink and made my excuses. He helped me harness the mare again, and asked if I cared to return, perhaps in a few days. Confused, I said that if business permitted I might drive this way. I could not be certain, I added.

And that was my introduction to Julian St Claire.

I did return, of course. I had no business, save portioning out my army pension and the small inheritance of my sister and I each month. I had no friends as such, and besides, St Claire intrigued me. I had no doubt that I was missing something, that beneath what I had seen there was a further truth to be revealed. That I had no idea what that truth might be only spurred me on.

The next week I made a brief visit, to assure myself of the place and my welcome. Both were certain. Then came a long afternoon, and a fuller introduction to his garden.

He was affable, and on the surface little more than a plantsman indulging a slightly peculiar preference for species of a toxic nature. Why should he not, when others obsessed over ferns, or tulips? I thought all such gardeners a little odd.

We walked his domain under a strong sun, drinks in hand.

"These diffenbachia, often called dumb-cane for good reason." He knelt on the gravel and displayed the broad leaves. "They cause an intense sensation of burning in the mouth, and the tongue can swell to such dimensions that you are indeed struck dumb."

"Is it fatal?"

I leaned on my stick, watching him intently. The gentle stroking of each plant; the way in which he plucked small shreds of a leaf and slipped them into his mouth, like a chef sampling herbs for a fine banquet. Today's drink had a different, headier aroma than before, and a sourness which fought the crushed sugar around the glass's rim. I had not tasted anything quite like it.

"Often." He stood up. "But it lets us communicate, for a moment, with mortality and what might lie within our souls."

We returned to the stone bench near the house.

"I do not truly comprehend, Mr. St Claire." I toyed with my glass, not meeting his eyes. "You say that each plant in your garden, every plant, flows with poisons, and yet you are unaffected."

"Unaffected?" I knew by the tone that I had made a mistake. "How could that be possible, sir? I said that I understood this place and what it holds. It affects me deeply."

"Forgive me, this is… new to me. I am no scientist, though I have tried to follow some of the more interesting themes of our age."

A silence for a moment, or rather a silence that was human. Birds called around us, and insects thronged in the garden, nectar and pollen everywhere for their industries. I wondered not to find them dying in their thousands, the gravel mingled with bee and wasp, hoverfly and butterfly, their wings feeble with toxins.

"Bog rosemary and mountain laurel do attract the pollinators," said St Claire. "And there is the jessamine, of course."

He must have noticed my gaze on the bees which surrounded a nearby specimen of an especially floriferous shrub.

"The jessamine?"

"Aromatic and beautiful, but it can be quite toxic to those who visit its flowers. Even the jessamine vines are said to have the potency of hemlock. My bees have learned, or died. Each year they grow stronger, the queens more attuned to the garden."

"Mr Darwin's evolutionary theories in action."

He thought on this.

"In a way, I suppose. They have many generations in only a few years, unlike ourselves. They change quickly."

Rested, we strolled again, down to the shallow stream which ran in the shadow of the far wall. Culverts allowed its entrance and its exit, while its length was populated with plants which loved shade and moisture. All, again, were quite poisonous, I had been told.

"Did your... your parents have a similar interest?"

A dead fish, three inches long and silver-white, floated in the weak current, a passing stranger only.

"No. This is my own work." He plucked a leaf of water hemlock and sucked on it, his eyes on the tiny corpse as it headed for the western culvert. "I was orphaned young, and raised by an aunt who took up residence here. She too died, when I was seventeen."

"By poison, I suppose." Nervous still, I laughed. He did not.

"She mistook her herbs," he said, as the fish was washed under a clump of feathery herbs which seemed much the same as the hemlock, if shorter.

"Water dropwort," he informed me. "Also known as the sardonic herb. It was given to the old, criminal, and insane in parts of Italy, to dispose of them. Risus sardonicus, the result of ingesting poor, unassuming Oenanthe crocata."

"The... the rictus smile? I thought that was associated only with death?"

"It can be survived." He bared his teeth in a mock grin. "We are all Sardinians in my garden."

I left not long after, claiming a dinner engagement. It was possible that Julian St Claire was unhinged, even a murderer if I considered the comment about his aunt. But I had never looked into eyes as large and strange as his, a face which so engaged me. I knew that men might love each other, even lie with each other—there had been a trooper in Texas who had suggested such things—but the attraction here was not physical.

I did not know what it was, not then.

I tried to talk to my sister that evening.

"His is an intellectual pursuit, from what little you tell me, Hervey." Her fork clattered against her plate, dislodging hard, stubborn peas. "A study of botany is all well and good, but this Mr. St Claire sounds a touch fanatical."

I felt that her words were harsh. "He is an aesthete, I suppose."

Mariella laughed. "An aesthete? Oh, Hervey. If he were to help you write a book on poisons, or learn cultivation, he would be a useful acquaintance." She gestured to the damp stain on the wall where the roof was leaking once more. "Becoming an aesthete will not pay for this."

It was ironic that whilst I had ridden, albeit briefly, with the US cavalry, and had travelled most of the southern states, my sister was the more wordly-wise of us. I decided to say no more of St Claire at that point.

Other visits to the Jessamine Garden, as I now called it, followed. St Claire introduced me to so many plants that I lost count. It seemed that there truly was nothing within those pale brick walls which could not kill. Cattle grazing there would have been dead within the day, men within the hour. But the garden was less strange than the man. I was still fascinated as to how St Claire could be so unaffected by the poisons with which he surrounded himself. He seemed to avoid the subject at first, preferring to introduce me to other corners of his realm.

"Here, my friend." He pointed to an attractive plant with many small leaflets. "Jequirity, or Indian licorice. Also know as the jumbie bead. If even a morsel of the small red seed is swallowed it can bring convulsions, and some of the Caribbean folk take this to be a sign that a jumbie, or evil spirit, has entered the person. Others say to the contrary, claiming that it wards off the jumbie."

"You have tried it?"

He looked at me, a slow smile forming on moist lips. "Of course. There is nothing here that I have not tried."

"Yet you seem... in good health."

"Never better. But I understand the direction of your thoughts. Do you truly want to learn more?"

I assured him that I did.

"Then you must have experience, for intellectual exploration is a dry thing."

"I must take poison?"

"No, not at all. I have few visitors since my aunt died. I would hardly seek to kill them, would I?"

I could not answer that, but essayed a faint smile of my own.

"Sit with me, then," he said.

An old log lay near the jequirity, and I eased myself down next to him. The afternoon sun had raised crickets and other insects in the long grass by the gravel—darnel or poison rye-grass, of course. St Claire was consistent in his plantings. The insects strummed and buzzed according to their types as St Claire rolled up his sleeves.

"Trust me." His pupils were wide, despite the sun, almost eclipsing the pale blue irises of his eyes. "Let me show you a little, just a little more..."

Flexing his long fingers, he touched the back of my hand with two fingertips. Heat again, but not so intense. I waited, dry-mouthed, for something to...

"Oh." I felt my heart flutter, its beat suddenly unreliable, and a sense of nausea. A rash had already appeared where he was touching me, but more alarming was the inner disquiet, that sensation when you first feel fear—or love, I imagine. Even despite my alarm I did not pull away. My pulse raced, then slowed, raced again. I knew that in some way I was being poisoned, yet I was also experiencing Julian St Claire. Beneath his pale skin he was a fire of blood, laced with such chemicals as I could not imagine, a raging presence in a slim, quiet body.

He withdrew his fingers. Two lines of painful blisters had formed across the back of my hand, radiating from where he had touched me. My pulse settled, faster than it had been but once more under a degree of control.

"What... what are you, sir?" I gasped.

He shrugged, smiled. "Only a man, with a garden. I make no other claims. What should I say about myself? If I stub my toe, it hurts. If I wield a pruning knife poorly, it cuts me. And now I am thirsty, like any man in this long summer. Come."

He took me into the house, and in a barely furnished room which looked out onto the garden, he gave me lemonade which tasted sweeter than it should, a shot of bourbon with that same herb as before. This time it tasted less bitter, and I finished it quickly.

"The blisters will worsen exposed to light," he said as I hobbled to the buggy. "You may wish to stay in the shade for a while."

Mariella noticed my hand at dinner, though I had tried to keep it turned from her.

"You've been at St Claire's again." Her words were light, her lips disapproving. "I asked about him in town. The locals will not take his paper money. The stores insist on hard coin that can be washed before circulation again."

I pretended indifference, but she was persistent.

"Miss Catchall at the milliners says that he carries some taint. They talk of cholera or the pox, though they cannot be sure."

The chicken was stringy, the beans picked too late to be crisp. I looked up from my plate.

"Gossip, Marie. Gossip about a single man who doesn't engage with the ladies, doesn't throw his place open for empty dances and chatter. I've shared drinks with him, had time in his house and his garden. I think that I'd know by now if I had picked up some unspecified plague."

"And your hand?"

"His plants are unusual. I strayed too close to something whose sap is an irritant. I was fully warned, and foolish."

"Yes. Foolish."

She did not play the piano that evening, merely sat embroidering in silence. It was her way of showing disapproval.

I went back, of course. He was always there, long dark hair swept back from his face and eyes which seemed to see so much more than mine. I had to think hard about my encounter with the trooper in Starr County to assure myself again that I was not in any way physically interested in St Claire. I do not think I was, but his quiet intensity could make me tremble, and his touch brought sensations which were entirely new to me.

One cooler morning he took me closer to the jessamine, had me breathe in its scent and let the air around it fill my lungs. Gently he pressed his fingers to my bare neck.

"Be brave, my friend," he whispered.

My skin burned, my back arched. This time it was not only my heart but the larger muscles of my arms and legs which responded to his touch, a tetany which almost felled me. My weak leg, ironically, was the one which held me upright, for the other locked and then spasmed. He kept me there, his hands at my neck, and through the fire I saw more of myself than ever before.

Pain, and sight through pain, self-knowledge. I knew the damage in my hip as I had never known it before, the minutiae of clumsily-healed bone and misplaced vessels. I traced the flawed muscle of my polio-afflicted leg, and found new things to consider—a slight enlargement of the liver, a knot of tissue round a healed rib, though I had never known that it had been broken.

I cried out, but not with words. Were we all such a complexity, such a wonder, if we could see as deeply into ourselves as this?

I do not know if it was his presence, his touch connecting me to him, which provided this sensation, or if some drug coursed through me. In Mexico they had talked of certain drinks, and the exudations of cacti, which made man hallucinate. St Claire had never spoken of such matters, nor did he use anything beyond a shot of bourbon, to my knowledge.

"Enough now," he murmured.

He eased me down onto one of the many logs by the path, and let go. The feeling of knowing myself was subsiding as rapidly as it had come, replaced by the acute discomfort of the areas where his fingers had lain against my bare flesh. I reached up with one hand and gingerly touched my neck. My fingers came away moist with watery blood.

"Perhaps we should not do this," he said, caressing a jessamine vine. "I ask too much of you."

"I do not... I do not know." I could barely speak.

He went to the house and procured a bandanna, which he wrapped gently around my neck, before offering me a double shot of rye whiskey.

"Rest before your journey home."

And so I remained there for almost an hour, listening to his occasional remarks on the properties of this plant and that—the sedative effects of baneberry, the many symptoms of poisoning by laburnum, all manner of common and uncommon botanical curiosities....

Mariella knew where I had been. She tore away the bandanna, gasped, and sent Susie, our maid, to fetch the doctor from town.

"You are a fool," she said, and stamped into the kitchen to boil water.

I looked in the hall mirror, and saw for myself. Five lines of angry pustules on either side of my neck, surrounded by a raised, blotchy area of skin. Some of the pustules had burst, weeping a thin, bloody fluid which had soaked into my collar. The pain was surprisingly bearable, though it worsened when I turned my head.

The doctor came within the hour. He was an elderly man with a long, old-fashioned beard. I had seen in him in town once or twice, and had asked him for laudanum for my hip, which he had supplied. We had never spoken more than a few words, though I knew him for a local man.

"I woulda said poison ivy, seein' as the skin's come up so," he muttered after examining me in my bedroom. "But it's mor'n that, ain't it, and the pattern, fahv marks on each side…"

"An experiment," I said, wincing as he touched my neck. "A… a friend of mine. We were examining the medical potential of some native plants…"

"Around yo' neck?" He paused, clicked his tongue in thought. "I would desist in them damn-fool experiments at once, leave 'em to men as knows. You'll maybe have permanent scarrin', young fellah."

But he applied a soothing cream over the area and bandaged my neck with care. I over-paid him, asking that he not expose my foolishness to the town. He weighed the coins in his hand, and nodded.

"Yo' business, Mistah Crane. Yo' business."

I listened to neither the doctor nor my sister. Even as they tended me, I wondered what it might be like to know what strangenesses lay inside the two of them, to sense them as I had sensed myself.

A fever came that evening, though it passed in less than a day. When I could move my neck without undue pain, I returned to the Jessamine Garden.

I realised that St Claire must have an unnatural awareness of his own body's construction and processes—perhaps of his very life-force. Through his hands, somehow, had flowed that awareness. And yet his touch was also poison to others, most literally. Would the one increase and the other lessen with exposure?

"You must tell me, St Claire." We stood under intertwined jessamine vines while bees, so much better adapted than myself, made play between the small trumpet-shaped blossoms. "How can this… condition of yours, this gift even, be possible?"

He frowned. "I thought you kindred in exploring sensation, yet you play scientist. I am not here to be investigated or categorised, Mr Crane."

He did not like my questions. A few days ago I had been 'Hervey' or 'my friend'.

"But there will be scientific reasons, surely…"

"You over-intellectualise, a habit you cannot seem to break." He shook his head wearily. "I am my garden. It courses in my arteries and veins. I propagate what you call poisons along each channel of my nerves, toxins slipping from one ganglion to the next and bringing new sensations. Each day is different."

He explained, though I was lost in the rush of his words, how time spent with the different genera brought changes which reflected the plants' own properties.

"There are the cardiac stimulants and arrestants, which flood the chambers or constrict them, so that the blood is flushed into hidden places. The foxglove, henbane, aconite and various lianas are ripe with possibilities in this area. You do not know what things I have seen in the grip of such palpitations—"

"But surely this is marvellous," I interrupted him. "The medical men of letters, they must be told of your insights."

I had disappointed him again.

"Medical men? The more I am exposed to my plants, the more I discard those outdated defences which my body once possessed. I accept their ways, embrace them. This is hardly useful to your doctors in their fine laboratories."

Committed to my obsession with enquiry that day, I could not stop myself from continuing, though I knew that I should say no more. I was a child, who asks one too many question and is at last slapped in frustration.

"You do not believe, then, that another who did this could become similarly resistant—"

He turned suddenly, a hard set to his narrow jaw.

"Resistant? Do you not listen to me, sir? Those who resist, die. Those who open their arms to new experiences, new intrusions into their being, are open to be changed, improved."

"I meant only that—" I raised my hands in entreaty.

"You should go," he said. "I forgive you, because the mistake is mine. I thought I had by chance found a mind which could understand, if only momentarily, my garden."

There was no reasoning with him. I left, chastened and confused.

I did not visit the Jessamine Garden for two weeks, during which I chopped wood, as best I could, and saw to some minor repairs on the house. My sister was pleased; I was eaten up with doubt and frustration. At night I felt my skin burn, and longed to experience myself again as I had with St Claire.

At last, unable to restrain myself, I harnessed up the mare. Mariella was visiting a cousin in Richmond, and I could not miss this opportunity.

St Claire was solicitous of my health, in a distant way. He seemed less inclined to do more than share a julep and general conversation. When he seemed on the point of ending our time there, I slid awkwardly to my knees.

"I surrender to you, sir," I said. Half the Venetian jug had been drained, mostly by myself, and I was awash with both fear and bourbon.

He tilted his head, and the dark centres of his eyes seemed to widen.

"What exactly are you saying?"

"I am saying that I surrender to your mystery, sir. I abandon my foolish questions, and beg that you let me understand, in such ways as you alone choose."

I held out my hands in reconciliation. He seemed to be considering, then took my hands in his, very lightly, our palms scarcely touching.

"Very well—Hervey," he said, soft-voiced once more.

I felt a burning sensation where his moist skin brushed mine, but I did not reject it. The sound of insects diminished, and I shuddered as my heart beat wild and unregulated, as my muscles cramped. I tasted salt-blood and bitterness in my mouth...

"Unhh!" I gripped his hands with perverse determination.

Do not think that this was pleasure. I had not felt such pain since the bullet slammed against my pelvis, but what came with the pain... such insights! I seemed to hear the rustle of every leaf and stem around me, even as I saw into myself again and heard the pump of fluids through my kidneys, the mad rhythm of my own heart. And beneath those, a sound like the throng at Jacksonville railway station, a thousand upon thousand murmurs which were my blood cells forcing their way through narrower and narrower channels...

He pried my fingers free and sat back. There were beads of sweat on his brow and smooth upper lip, a slight tremble to his shoulders.

"I believe that you see now, a little at least."

"Is there… is there more?" I managed to say.

"More? There is everything, yet."

"Please, do not spare me. To go this far…" I held up my hands again, one arm still twitching uncontrollably.

And now he seemed the reluctant one, glancing at his garden, then back at me with huge eyes.

"A promise, then," he said at last. "Or a warning."

He placed one index finger on his lower lip, and let saliva form there. I knelt, shaking, as he extended his arm and pressed the same finger to my own lips.

Skin brushed against skin had shocked me. The taste of his clear, bitter-sweet saliva brought lightning down. My body stiffened, immovable and in that brief contact I felt the garden with such intensity that I thought I might be blinded.

There were colours around me which surely had not been there before—a burning, golden umber where there had been mere brown bark, sullen reds which veined formerly green leaves—all manner of things which I could not explain. The yellow jessamine flowers outshone the morning sun, almost too much to look at. The air, the air was both sharp and thick at the same time, wave after wave of perfumes which made you wish to retch, which made you beg for yet another gulp of them. This was a chaos of sensation which went beyond my ability to record.

And we were there within the lightning storm—Julian St Claire, solid and as one with it; Hervey Crane in a spasm of experience, barely able to breath. We were alive in a way which I had never understood until that moment…

"Enough," he said, lifting a glass of julep to my lips and washing away his taint. His gift.

I closed my eyes, let my heart settle. My lips and cheeks were burning, swollen, and jagged pains ran down the cords of my neck. I knew that the half-healed blisters on my neck had opened and were weeping, but did not care. Could not care, in the face of what had happened to me.

It was some time before I could see or co-ordinate enough to take the reins of the buggy. He offered nothing, no further help except water for my dry, painful thirst, but those eyes were on me, I know, until I was well beyond normal sight.

I am closing my journal, ending it after this entry.

Mariella sits brooding in the corner of the room. Kid-skin gloves prevent her from the retreat to her beloved piano. She went to St Claire's place this morning, and came back pale, one hand cracked and blistered.

She had slapped him, apparently, told him that he must turn me away if I came back to that "unholy" garden of his. He had said nothing, merely taken her blow and left, lost amongst the jessamine vines. The swellings on her right hand and wrist are subsiding quite quickly, but she cannot yet co-ordinate enough to play her scales, let alone Mozart.

The doctor attended to her hand after he had seen to my more serious blisters and lesions. One side of my face will not move, as if it had been whipped with nettles and poison oak, and my neck still bleeds. I am in pain, sedated and heavily bandaged, as I said, but I feel only the promise of what is to come.

In the morning, before Mariella awakes, horse and buggy will take me to the Jessamine Garden. I will drink his bitter julep, and I will take his face in my bare hands, press my lips hard to his and taste the fullness of Julian St Claire. In that moment, I believe that I will truly know what lies beneath our shallow skins.

I do not imagine that I will return.

John Linwood Grant lives in Yorkshire with a pack of lurchers and a beard. He may also have a family. When he's not chronicling the adventures of Mr. Bubbles, the slightly psychotic pony, he writes a range of supernatural, horror and speculative tales, some of which are actually published. You can find him every week on greydogtales.com, often with his dogs.

SUBSUME

JOANN OH

The possessions begin the same way, strapped down in your dark cell. A pain in your temples—sharp and jagged if it's one of the newborns, dull if it's a full Daughter—pushing in at the edges of your consciousness. It's nearly a relief when you break and she floods in. Her fingers worm into each crevice in your mind until every synapse has been worked over. A newborn is clumsy, scuffing and shoving so your neurons feel frayed. A Daughter is deft, but still her presence makes every nerve scream.

She always begins with Pep's burned face bursting after the hull breach, then works backward. Pep's ballooned skull deflates, his eyeballs coagulate as buckled alloy straightens and rejoins. Shards fly back into the navigational display and the compressor on Pep's suit repairs itself, his blistered skin smoothing. The energy-eating jets of their scythe-like ship disappear from your screens. Alarms quiet and stillness descends.

She doesn't skip over the dreary monotony of a deep-space slog in the cockpit of a Coalition freighter. The long, isolated hours. Pep's iciness every time you rotate shifts. Your rebuff. His advance, pressed against you by the terrarium then slowly sidling away. The brief flirtations decreasing in intensity. And then waking up from cryo in reverse, sinking backwards into sleep as Pep's face fades from your vision.

You get more of a sense of her in the long dark of cryo. Your memories go still and hers filter through the gap. The warmth of the larval cocoon, her sisters trembling around her, their consciousnesses bright points of light in the dim web of drone minds. Her limbs break into joints, tough exoskeleton creeping over her body. The cocoon thins as she hardens. She can hear the tapping of drone feet outside. Hunger stirs within her and she lunges, stabbing her many-jointed legs through her cocoon. She snatches the drone. Shoves its head into her mouth. Her mandibles puncture its bristly head capsule, sclerotic plates crumpling in a spurt of fluid. The drone's death screams vibrate against her maxilla as sweet hemolymph drips down her throat.

Her sisters are hatching and killing as well. She swallows the last of the still-twitching drone and stands, bulbous abdomen dragging the ragged remains of her larval sac. Still hungry, she shreds a neighboring cocoon and slaughters the barely moving nymph inside before lowering her mouthparts to feed. The carnage goes on until only a few of her sisters remain, clicking their mandibles and hissing as they circle warily around the larval pit. The bright constellation of unborn consciousness has coalesced into a few fierce stars.

Her memories end as the Mother enters her. The blaze of an ancient, inexorable mind pours through her psyche. She is subsumed. The surviving daughters cower in the gooey remains of their sisters. Those who resist are overwhelmed by drones and torn apart.

Beyond the hatching, you only catch hints of memory. Hunkering in the heart of the hive as male drones penetrate her one by one before she eats their heads. Eggs sliding from her ovipositor, lining the walls of the larval pit. Stepping out of the hive into the gloom of a dying sun. Phalanxes of drones—hers and the enemy's—swarming into each other, minds winking out as hemolymph sprays the ground. The images are faded, like a much-handled photograph or an off-planet transmission corrupted by radiation.

Then she gets back to the beginning of your cryo sleep and your memories scroll again. Unconsciousness seeps away, icy gas is sucked back into chambers. You climb out from your cryo cell and Pep winks at you through the hallway window.

Final health evaluations. Nurses draw serums from your arm as Pep jokes with you from one bed over.

She moves on to physical fitness trials. Toweling sweat back onto his head, Pep asks whose face you imagine on the leather bag as you pull back punch after punch, knuckles and wrists releasing their ache. You jog the track together, your reticence building as Pep's banter spools back into his mouth.

She always stops at the jogging. In the open air, grass bordering the track, sun high in a clear sky. As if she's seen enough. She withdraws, leaving your mind feeling flogged.

Usually, you pass out.

You're left in darkness between possessions. The air is moist and hot and sweat leaves a constant film on your naked skin. You don't know if you ever sleep. Your restraints are flexible, but you don't remember when you gave up struggling. You're fed, slimy tubes forced between your teeth and a viscous liquid pumped into your mouth until you gag. You void yourself from both ends and your excretions are mysteriously cleaned in the darkness. The only sounds you hear are your own breathing, moaning, puking, gagging. How long you've been there you don't know. How long since you were pulled from the wreckage of your ship, how long since you watched Pep's unhelmeted head explode, your screams reaching no further than your own ears. How long since the first possession.

There have been so many since then you almost forget how it was different. The first one penetrated your mind as smoothly as a syringe sliding into flesh. Like an anesthesiologist's drip you barely notice until you wake up groggy with the surgery already over.

She also began with Pep's death, but from there, ignored chronology. You were screaming, then the memory shifted. The alarms were gone and the interior lights dim. Pep's face was whole, bent towards yours as his hands slid down your waist. You turned away, told him no.

Shift. Night, outside the Coalition barracks. You were still saying no, but this time to a different man who forced you anyway.

Shift. Your legs were jelly beneath the weight of your pack, but you forced yourself to run the last hundred meters, forced yourself to stand until your commander dismissed you, forced yourself to walk off the others' taunts, until finally in the cool dark of the barracks you collapsed on your bunk.

Shift. Your sparring partner collapsed in the ring. You were smaller, but you beat her by striking first, striking hard, and striking over and over again. You walked away with blood smearing your knuckles.

Shift. He spat blood, sprawled in the dust. You gave him a taste of what would happen if he ever touched you again.

Shift.Shift.Shift.

She sifted through your life, your memories running through her feelers like sand. When she was done, you were taken into your cell, stripped down, and strapped in. From then on, you were given to Daughters and newborns for practice, each following the same dogged route like obedient schoolchildren. The first never possessed you again.

Why they're doing this to you, you have no idea. You barely have the mental energy to wonder before another one of them possesses you. They feed you, wash you, possess you.

Again and again and again.

Maybe you sleep. How else do you explain the nightmares?

Pep's head bursts, but not because of the shattered navigational display. Because he touched you. You shred his suit like a larval sac and space's vacuum sucks him out. He spits blood. You drink it.

When will it stop?

Will it ever stop.

You're losing your edges, of where you stop and where they begin. Where she begins. She begins where Pep ends. She begins by consuming her sisters.

She begins to consume you.

Pep's face burns. You spurn him. You climb into your cell and sink into the deep sleep of cryo. She hatches.

A newborn pulls out of your mind, leaving you gagging on your own vomit. She was worse than most, jerking through your consciousness like a newly hatched nymph tearing out of her cocoon. You retch and warm liquid dribbles from your mouth.

It's sweet, like hemolymph.

Hunger stirs in your gut. How long since the feeding tubes were last shoved down your throat? The restraints are gone, replaced by a taut material wrapped over your body and head, forcing your chin to your chest. You breathe into a pocket of stale air in the space above your sternum. There's no way you can eat like this. You try to straighten, to push against the covering. It stretches, your fingers poking through thin membrane.

Outside, your sisters are hatching.

Joann has lived in Indonesia, Malaysia, and the U.S., where she currently works as a graphic designer in Colorado. Travel, hikes, and pottery are some of her loves. The fastest way to her heart: Buy her a bowl of pho.

Rig Rash

Victoria Dalpe

The way I hear it, the day they found oil was the day the town of Sanctuary was both saved and ruined.

Black Gold.

We flocked in like vampires to an open wound. First, the prospectors to confirm it was true; then the money men in expensive suits and slick black cars with their schemes to profit, profit, profit. Then the laborers, going where the work was. And once the laborers hit, well, then it was an explosion. Fast food chains, all; hotels, motels and flop houses sprung up like rashes along the southern corner of town. Fellas get lonely out in the oil fields, need some company. That's where I came in.

I'd been hitching, moving from town to town, working truck stops and the occasional motel room gig. But since I refused to work for a pimp I couldn't stay anywhere too long without it involving some kinda altercation or violence, sometimes to them, most of the time to me. There are reasons most places don't like free agents. And let's be honest, I was getting a little long in the tooth. I'm not old, but I'm no spring chicken or tween bride.

Anyway, I was a few hundred miles farther south than I'd ever been before, plying my trade for a ride and a meal when I caught the first whiff of Sanctuary.

He was a Big Burly Man, red beard and red nose, stinking of sweat and sour mash. He spoke low and in circles. Like drunks do. His faux whisper carried across the whole room and right to my ears.

"I told my boss I wasn't going back there, no matter how much he'd pay me. Not about the fucking money! I mean money, yeah. Sure. Great. But... there's something wrong up there, people are getting sick. You go on up if you want to, man, but if you're smart you'd steer clear. Some things are better than money."

I disagreed with him there; not much better than money as far I was concerned. And I thought to myself, *If Sanctuary's a town with jobs aplenty and those jobs are hard dirty jobs, then it's the kind of place that could probably use a few more women.*

You are probably wondering, *What did I think of his warnings? I didn't think of them at all.* Everything makes you sick these days. The air is poison, the sea is poison. The burger I was eating as I eavesdropped—probably making me sick.

Plus, I figured, if something's making people sick, it'll be in the ground. I'm not going to go into the ground. I'm going into the wallets of the people who're in the ground—and, if I'm lucky, the people who hire those people.

So I thumbed my way farther south. Imagine me there, on the side of the highway, dollar signs in my eyes. A duffel and a dream.

A guy named Steve drove me the last leg of the way. He was an oil worker himself, heading back to Sanctuary.

Steve didn't want sex. In fact, he was a real family man. Headed back to Sanctuary after seeing his wife and kid back in Indiana. When I asked why he didn't bring them to live in Sanctuary, his face twitched, pinched up, clenched.

"Boomtown's no place for families. For decent people." He gave me a sidelong glance.

I thought, *Shit, Steve, you're headed the same place I am.*

He dropped me off on the corner of Main St. then drove off, no doubt thinking only decent thoughts.

The town of Sanctuary was about as ugly as a small town could be; "quaint" taken to a horrific extreme. The air smelled of sulfur and chemicals, the gentle breeze caused my eyes to water.

The road was cracked old pavement and the sidewalks were vacant, save a few rats sticking to the shadows.

I had walked a block or two, trying to decide which bar might hold the man lucky enough to provide me a place to sleep for the night and pay for that privilege. A lone woman in a town like this, even a savvy one like myself, had to be smart and careful. Too many landfills are filled with women in my line of work, women that are too often seen as disposable.

"You lost honey?" The voice startled me, it bounced off empty buildings and echoed. I spun, and a man pulled himself from the alley and staggered toward me. As he drew nearer I could see his skin was red with rash. I instinctively stepped back.

"Aww, don't be like that honey, just thought you might need a little company." I took another step back.

"I'm fine buddy, you just startled me is all." The man had a strange smell about him, the closer he got, the stronger it got. Oil, solvents and... fishy?

He stepped beneath a streetlight and I saw that the rash was much worse than I initially thought. Angry welts and deep black furrows covered his face. His eyes were yellow, boiled-looking. And the stink of him was overpowering. I covered my nose with my sleeve.

"It's the smell innit?" He said, offended at my revulsion, "It's the oil pits you know. Gets in your gloves, in your boots. In your masks. Like it wants... to be in you. You can wash and wash but it sticks. Taste it in my food. You'll get there soon enough. Then you won't look at me like you do..."

"There a problem out here?" A big man with an unlit cigarette called out from behind me. "Bill Higgins, get your ass home and take a shower. And stop scaring off tourists, we're lucky to have a lady in town."

The Big Man's name was Patrick and he had come to Sanctuary after working in oil in Texas and Louisiana. He drove a nice black truck and owned a small trailer outside of town, with a small square of land he'd filled with bikes and a big dog house and kennel.

"You have a dog?" I asked casually as he opened the door and helped me out of his truck.

His face darkened and he shook his head.

Later. After our business was done and he was serving me up some dinner, he told me more. He'd had two dogs when he moved to Sanctuary. Big dogs, one a Rottweiler and the other a German Shepard. Smart, companionable dogs that had lived their lives on oil fields.

But Sanctuary got to them. They would never sleep, paced all night, whining and whining. Started picking at hotspots, gnawing themselves red and raw. Rash all over. They became skeletal, crazy, dangerous.

And then he said a pack of rats attacked the dogs, managing to chew a hole to something vital in one. And leaving the other frothing and injured. He put that one down himself.

"Rats?" I said incredulously. He shrugged, indifferent whether I believed or not.

Guys who work on oil rigs tend to have pets to keep them company on the road Patrick told me.

"Oil fields breed lonely men. And lonely men like the company of dogs, and they are cheaper than you lot," he said. But none of the animals lasted long in Sanctuary. They'd go crazy, run off, get bitten up by vermin or just drop dead.

"Something in the water," he joked humorlessly, and I set the glass I was about to drink down.

———————

Eventually I did drink the water. It had a faint foulness to it, though it could have been my imagination. Like smelling the milk after its "sell by" date, it always smells sour. The physical and the psychological start to blend and it's hard to tell what is real.

Sanctuary was like that. How much was anecdotal, hearsay about bad luck, bad health, bad water—and how much was more than that? And more importantly, what kept us all there?

I thought about leaving that first night after Patrick. But I'm stubborn, always have been. Ever since I slammed the door on my mom's face back in my teens. Maybe I just lacked sense, maybe we all did.

———————

Still River Motel was located just off the main drag. It had exactly the unsavory reputation I needed for my business.

The night manager's name was Quentin. He looked how you'd expect: pasty, soft, shiny on top, ponytail down the back and dark circled eyes. Repulsive, but pleasant enough. After some business discussion, he agreed to provide me with a room and himself with a foggy memory.

The room was disgusting. No one would ever say I was a lady with refined taste, but I do like sheets that don't peel apart like a grilled cheese sandwich. So I set about tidying and beautifying before I started welcoming customers.

It was in the process of laying a plastic sheet beneath those provided by the hotel, that I came across the stain.

Now, there are many genres of motel room stains. I don't need to go into the types, colors and causes. I'm sure you can figure them out. Well, this stain was black. Black like ink. And as big as a man. I'd never seen a stain like that before.

I stared at it disgusted and fascinated, and then started trying to get rid of it. After scrubbing with water and cleaner did little, I tried flipping the mattress over, double sheeting it, and then lying down. But like a tell tale heart hammering beneath the floorboards, I couldn't relax knowing it was there. I always knew that it was under me.

Did someone coated in oil lay down on the bed? Was it a fetish, some sort of black gold body massage thing? Had a fire caused it? Mold? What?

And that's when I noticed the smell. It was subtle but once noticed, undeniable. That stain stunk. Fishy, chemical, foul. It stunk so bad I had to crack the windows.

I begged but eventually paid for Quentin to give me a new mattress. Saw him drag this "new" mattress out of the room next door. This new one stunk, too, but just of BO. And it was riddled with familiar stains: yellow, red, brown.

But mercifully, no black.

A few days in, and I was working steady. That's when there was a knock on my door. It was a standard knock, the nervous rat-a-tat-tat of a john looking for action.

I peered through my peephole. Outside, a man with his head turned away from the door.

"Yeah?" I said, wary. I did not like the way he moved foot to foot, looking up and down the hall.

"Looking for a friend, a lady friend, this the right room?"

My guts told me to say no, but my head told me money's money. So I opened the door.

He burst into the room, radiating nervous energy. Wired. He wouldn't make eye contact; he paced the room like a cat.

"My friend is coming, don't lock the door."

"Your friend?" My mind went to the knife I kept hidden under my pillow. But you have to be careful with a knife. Draw it when it's not necessary and pretty soon it will become necessary.

He told me his name was Owen. So Owen and I waited.

A moment later another knock. Owen let another man in. This guy was still, silent, hood up and face a mess of stubble. I glanced at the phone and wondered if I should be calling the night manager.

Owen followed my glance. "Nothing sketchy Miss, we promise," He said in a flurry, his eyes too wide. "This is my buddy, Peter." The hood just grunted a nod.

"You're prettier than the other girl, who used to use this room." Owen said, then looked away, embarrassed. I noticed the way he scratched at his arms, like a dog with fleas.

"What other girl?" I asked, mouth going dry, finding Owen's endless movement and Peter's stillness equally unsettling.

"Never mind. Doesn't matter."

Turns out that Owen was a watcher and Peter was a doer. I don't mind a little weird stuff as long as the price is right. The price here was right.

At first, it was just bad sex. Peter kept all his clothes on, even the hood. He didn't so much mount as he did crawl atop me. I noticed immediately the chemical smell of oil, and the dirt under his fingernails.

As Peter started getting his money's worth, Owen settled into the only chair in the room, already working himself with efficiency.

Mercifully it was all over fast. Peter came almost silently. His body went rigid for a moment, then he slid off of me.

As he pulled up his pants, I noticed the red rashy skin on his thighs. He saw what I saw and averted his eyes, ashamed? He dropped the rubber in the trash beside the bed.

And then Owen came. A spurt of black on the carpet. Black like oil. The kind of black you don't want to see on the business end of someone's dick.

A pearlescent black puddle.

I stared at it. He stared at me staring at it.

"I didn't touch you. No harm right?"

"Get the fuck out, and never come back," I screamed.

As the door closed behind them, I scrambled to the trashcan and looked in, breathed out a sigh of relief when I saw the condom.

After the longest, hottest shower on the planet, I tried and failed to get some sleep. Images of the black stain coming back again and again unbidden. The puddle of black jism glistening on the carpet under a washcloth haunting me.

I went to Quentin that night. Stomped down to his greasy little booth in little more than a nightgown and a scowl that could strip paint of a building.

"Tell me about the other girl, the one who used to work my room."

Quentin hemmed and hawed, but finally caved, as weak willed men always do.

"She was crazy, a junkie. She started saying something was burning her inside, from the inside out. Then one day she came down clawing at herself and wailing, wanted help, wanted me to call an ambulance."

"And then?"

"Then nothing. I told her to sober up or she would end up in jail or rehab. Sent her back to her room." Quentin paused then, a ghost of something crossing his face, regret perhaps. "Then she killed herself, or tried to cut it out of herself and died, or something like that. She was nuts. I dunno, I mean she was a dirty crackhead. It happens."

"On my mattress?" I asked, mouth dry. "'Cuz that was not blood all over it."

He shrugged, "Not your mattress any more. Not your problem neither."

———————

After that I decided it was better to sever my business ties with the Still Water Motel and its standard clientele. Step it up a notch.

I found the perfect location between the main drag and the oil fields. Old widow lived in the main house. Mostly deaf, and kind in her own way. She was just happy to see another woman in town, and she wanted us to stick together. If she knew my occupation, she seemed indifferent to it. I paid the rent, and she asked no questions. Word was she used to be a cat lady, and her house did have that faint pissy odor. But they had all run off or died off, as all the pets of Sanctuary seemed to do.

As for the working girl in the motel? I asked around here and there, and learned that yes, she was a crackhead, and yes, I was much prettier, and that yes, she did kill herself. But the details of that suicide were sketchy. Some said she cut her wrists, others said she disemboweled herself, and still others said, that she tried to cut out her own womb because something was growing in there. But it was because she was crazy and a tweaker, not because there was anything inside to actually cut out.

Or so they insisted.

I upped my rate. I became a lot more discerning in my clientele. Referrals only. Showers before business, and I would inspect the goods. I was greedy but I wasn't suicidal.

———————

I started having a recurring dream. In it I was sitting in a bathtub, staring at my toes as they peeped out of the water. Outside the window, the sky churned, and green clouds streaked past, faster and faster. A warm, sickly wind fluttered the curtains and brought with it the noxious stink of sulfur, and the chemical burn of solvents.

I would watch as black fluid seeped from between my legs. It unfurled like ink in water, like smoke. Oil: sticky and viscous. Foul smelling. I stand and a great gush empties from my womb, painting my legs black. I scream and it pours from my mouth, burning, the foulest substance in all creation, pure liquid death.

I noticed a rash on Patrick, the regular with the dead dogs, one night as he washed up. It was on one shoulder blade, in that hard to reach spot, the one back scratchers were invented for.

"What's that?" I asked voice trembling, but I knew all the same. Patrick was one of my favorite customers.

"Oh yeah, just Rig Rash, or Pit Rash, whatever you want to call it."

He slid his shirt on and averted his eyes. "You ever get it on other oil fields? Outside of Sanctuary?" His face darkened and he shook his head. "Only here."

A moment later he added: "All the guys here get it eventually."

And he was right about that. More and more of my clients came in with blotches of angry rash, reminding me of poison ivy on steroids. The worse it got, the more it weeped—blackish and streaked with pus. It stunk, they stunk.

I took to washing all my linens in bleach and practically scouring myself after every interaction. I filled the apartment with potpourri and scented candles. But even still, my small abode took to stinking like everything else in the town of Sanctuary.

You may be wondering why I didn't pack it in right then. Truth is: Folks were sick but I'd never had so much cash in hand in my whole life.

But yeah. It was wearing on me. The long days of strange pea soup skies and stinking hot air, the longer nights of bad dreams and sheets that never got clean, started to get to me. I stared at myself one morning, looking into my reflection, wondering how far it would have to go for me to leave, or if I even could if I wanted to. I dreaded the answer.

Sitting at Merv's, one of the three main street bars one night, nursing a whiskey and waiting for a date, I was surprised to see another working girl come up and sit beside me, she ordered a vodka and soda and lit a cigarette, blowing out a plume of smoke before talking to me.

The woman, older than me, or perhaps just lived harder than me, was named Cheryl. She was from a neighboring pissant town and had come for the boom like we all had. Moths to the flame.

There are very few secrets between whores. And Cheryl's tale was something.

It all started when she agreed to go to a foreman's trailer out on a dig site one night for a little fun and birthday entertainment.

When she got there, three men were waiting outside, plus the one who drove her. Cheryl went in and they all proceeded to drink, and dance, and have a good time. Cheryl told me that she was bent over the desk, one of the gentleman riding her from behind when she saw something move in the corner of the room.

She screamed and called out, "I'm real afraid of vermin!"

She was sure it had gone to hide behind the file cabinet in the corner. The men, drunk and half dressed, indulged and one started to move the cabinet, while another held up a fire extinguisher as a weapon.

Beneath the cabinet was pitch black, a stain in the carpet. And at the center of the stain, was a hole in the floor. Made it look like the stain was eating its way through the floor, eating its way through the fiberglass insulation. Like something was trying to get in. Got in.

The men knelt looking at the strange stinking hole. The carpet squished and bubbled up black when one poked it with a pen. Cheryl was having none of it. She was ready to go. She began gathering her things, getting dressed.

Just then that a rat exploded from the hole, streaked across the room and scrambled up her body, attaching itself to her forearm. "Its body was slick with oil. It was soggy and it reeked and it— it…"

Then she pulled back her sleeve and showed me the wound. Her forearm was gnarled. A dark, nearly black, scab had formed over the gnaw marks. "It still bleeds sometimes," she said. "Never heals."

Back to the story: One of the men had finally pulled it off of her. Another had bashed it into pulp with the extinguisher. They all stood over it for a look. The rat, for it was indeed a rat, was horribly disfigured. Its body appeared more oil than fur, its blood was black, its organs tinged green.

They found a rats' nest under that damned trailer, hundreds and hundreds of them down there, living in the oil, fucking in it, swimming in it, dying in it.

Cheryl shrugged. "I been to the hospital." She'd received tetanus and rabies and various other shots, and stitches for the bite. "I may lose my arm, say the wound is necrotic," she said. "They don't know what's wrong with it."

My mind wandered, trying to find connections between all I had heard. "You know of another girl? Worked out of Still Water—that killed herself."

"You must mean Shelley. I used to think what everyone else thought: that she was drug addled and out of her mind. Y'know what I think now?

"Now I think there really was something in her. Just like she said there was."

A silence settled between us. And then Cheryl took my arm. Squeezed it hard and she looked me in the eyes. "Something is wrong in this town, and that wrongness is under our damn feet." She told me I could come with her if I wanted. But that, for sure, if I had any sense, I would leave town.

We parted ways not long after. I wished her luck. And I stayed, ignoring yet another warning.

———————————————

That night I got into the tub, trying to relax, to purge Cheryl's story, but—the dreams, the smells, the rats—it was getting to me. And it wasn't just the stories, it was the town itself. Sanctuary was a queer little place: there were no kids here, there were no pets, and I could not remember seeing the sun once since I arrived.

But was the oil really at fault for all of this? How could that even be? I was not a learned woman, but I took some biology and earth science in high school. I watched the news from time to time. If it was as bad as everyone said, even greed couldn't keep the town going. Right? And there must be regulations and water and air safety. Isn't that the EPA's job? I wanted to see the oil for myself.

Conveniently a john, ironically named John, agreed to drive me out to the oil fields the next night.

He was a nice enough fellow—young, optimistic, and not yet poisoned by the water and the land. New. He wanted to take me for a hamburger and have a real date, but I needed to wrap my head around Sanctuary, needed to see ground zero.

The Withers farm was long gone, and as far as the eye could see were large rotating pumps and drills, lazily spinning, reminding me improbably of dinosaurs. Above, the sky churned, and a sick feeling settled in my guts. That wrongness everyone kept telling me about, I could sense it all around me.

"This site is different, right? From other oil fields?" I asked John as we walked closer to the job site, the smell growing thicker with every step.

John chuckled then. Like I'd made a joke. But of course I hadn't made any joke.

"People do have some crazy theories."

"Humor me, sweetheart."

"Well one of the guys, he's up and gone now, said that this oil, this whole operation was like nothing he'd ever seen. The actual crude oil was different. He suggested, and I don't believe him necessarily, that was because the oil wasn't from the traditional fossils and organisms."

"I don't follow." My gut dropped.

"Well, oil's a fossil fuel right? Made up of ancient critters that died long, long ago, and after all the years of pressure from the rock and the heat, they become oil. But this guy thought the oil here all came from one dead creature. Not hundreds of dead dinosaurs or what have you. But a single one. Huge."

I looked down at my feet. Couldn't help it. And suddenly had the unsettling feeling that I wasn't standing on the ground. Instead I felt like I was on a boat, floating on an impossibly deep ocean.

"Something bigger than the whole town. He thinks it's down there now. Gigantic, a creature so big no one has ever heard of it. So big it can't be discovered. Can you imagine, all of this from one animal? That was the craziest theory I have heard so far about Sanctuary. But there is a weird poetry to it don't you think?"

That night I could not get John's words out of my head, a skittish part of my mind kept returning to it, trying to conjure what a creature like that would look like. Once asleep, I was haunted by dreams of black fluid pouring from me, and slimy-slick rats scrabbling in the walls, in the floors. All of us filled to the brim with corruption.

At 3 a.m., I woke and went for a glass of water. It was nearly to my lips when I caught my reflection and I dropped the glass to shatter in the sink. There on my clavicle, above the old camisole I wore to sleep in, was a patch of red rashy skin.

"Oh, fuck no," I whispered. I'd been careful, so fucking careful, but it didn't matter.

I felt along the rash's edges. The skin was hot and itchy as I prodded it. A sheen of pus came off on my fingertips, sticky. Stinking. It was tinged iridescent black in the bathroom light.

And this is what sounds craziest, as I prodded it, investigating the blasted Rig Rash, it moved.

The rash itself slithered across the bones of my clavicle and settled on my chest. Now, I know how that sounds. That sounds insane. But I swear to god. A saner woman may have gotten dressed and headed to the ER, but by that point I had been in Sanctuary for two months, and I was starting to believe that a hospital couldn't do shit for me. Hell, I did believe.

In a panic I stumbled into my kitchen, found the biggest damn knife I had, grabbed a jug of Clorox from beneath the pantry and got to work. With own my reflection to guide me, I cut the rash out off of me before it could move again.

Once I'd filleted myself, I flushed the tainted skin down the toilet—what else was I to do with it? I prayed to God, Buddha, Gaia, whoever, that I had gotten the infection out.

Then I dumped the bleach straight onto my bleeding, skinless chest. Bleach kills everything, after all.

The pain was indescribable.

Once I stopped screaming and the throbbing lessened to ohmygodohmy godohmygod, I packed my bags, "borrowed" my landlady's car and left her enough money to buy another with a brief note apologizing for leaving on such short notice. And then I bailed, my foot to the pedal all the way past town lines.

Real or imagined, I could still feel it inside me, leaking out, staining the wadded up bandages taped to my chest like a trail of squid's ink.

And to give you the long answer, that is why I've got this stinking bandage on my chest and a wound that won't fucking heal. And that's why I've had to knock precious dollars off my rate.

And that's why when you tell me you're headed up to Sanctuary I say, "Oh hell no." There's something in that boomtown getting fat on our greed and our disbelief. Something big and dead, or maybe not as dead as we'd like to think, and it's under our feet. Hell, it's in our cars, it's heating our fucking houses. It's in the air we breathe. I know how that sounds, believe me. But everything I told you is cut my heart out and hope to die true.

Listen, how about we go back to your room now. We transact a little business. I'll give you a good deal on account of the bandage and the disgusting tale I told you. Then we head south. I hear there's oil work in Louisiana. That's where I'm headed. You could go to Mardi Gras? Kiss dusky Creole girls. Stand on firm ground. Make the right kind of mattress stains.

Trust me. Sanctuary ain't worth it.

Victoria Dalpe is a writer and visual artist based out of Providence, RI where she lives with her husband, writer and filmmaker Philip Gelatt Jr. and their young son.

IRIDESCENT

SANDRA M. ODELL

Son, I want you to take me into town.

The fading thought floated through Willard's mind like milkweed down on the wind. He caught the pickle crock before it hit the floor, set it on the drain board by the sink pump, then hurried into the front room.

Willard's father lay on the davenport beneath a mound colorful quilts: Broken Star, Log Cabin, California Rose. Long gray fingers traced patterns worn smooth by years of such explorations. Solid black eyes stared out the window at the early summer day, at things Willard could not see, eyelids blinking from the bottom up.

He knelt by the broken down sofa. "Why? What's wrong?"

His father did not turn his head. *It is my time.*

The world opened up and swallowed Willard whole. He closed his eyes. "Are you...Are you sure?"

Everything dies, Son.

His father's thoughts curled through Willard like that first sip of how-come-you, but couldn't pull him out of the dark places the way they had as a boy.

A spindly gray arm came out from under the quilts and reached past Willard's shoulder. *Junior.*

The baby began to cry. Willard hurried to the cradle by the cold fireplace and took his infant son into his arms. "There now," he cooed, breathing in the sweet combination of talcum powder and lemon soap.

Willard Junior rubbed eager pink cheeks over his father's checkered shirt.

"I got none of that, little man, but Momma'll be back right shortly."

Let me see him one last time.

Willard laid his son atop the mound of quilts. His father touched a trembling, three-jointed finger to the baby's head and the crying stopped.

Willard Junior blinked solid black eyes, blinked a second time and they were baby blue. The babe hiccupped, blue eyes closed, and he began to snore.

He will learn many things, understand many more. Tell him he has always made me proud.

Willard gathered his son to his chest. "I will."

Try as he might, he couldn't keep the words from breaking on his grief.

Willard's father closed his eyes. His nostril flaps quivered with a sigh. *It is time.*

"Now? I can't leave Junior here without his momma, and—"

He will sleep until his mother arrives.

"Oh."

With a last look at his son, Willard set the boy in the cradle, collected his father from the sofa, and carried him to the truck outside. Wizened and frail, his father weighed next to nothing, less even than Willard Junior. Willard did not want to think about that, or how the afternoon sun shone through his father's hand resting on top of the quilts. The thoughts came anyway.

He opened the passenger side door and set his father on the cracked leather seat. The cab of the old Ford smelled like chicken feed and stale Pall Malls. "Want me to roll down the window so you can feel the wind?"

Yes.

Willard did, then climbed into the driver's seat. Key in the ignition, pump the gas three times, don't think, just do. The engine coughed once, twice, and rumbled to life. Wishing he had tear ducts, he eased the truck down the drive to Brown's road.

Willard felt his father's sad smile though the lipless mouth had never managed the expression. He turned onto the county road, the long way into town, buying himself precious minutes at eighteen cents a gallon. Rows of young alfalfa flickered by like lights in a movie house. "Where should I take you?"

Into town is fine.

Willard clutched the wheel. "People won't much like you coming into town."

No, they will not.

He hunched his shoulders against the chill clawing up his spine. "Let me turn around and call Doc Stokes, see what he says."

No.

"You know he won't mind."

His father set a four-fingered hand against the wind, molding the unseen the way he'd done all of Willard's life. "There's nothing magic to it," Ma used to say. "That's just Pa's way is all."

Ma said lots of things like that before God took her. Willard's father never said, only did.

I have lived a life without fuss. I see no need to change it now.

The truck rumbled past the lightning maple on the left hand side of the road, its bark scarred by dozens of strikes over its one-hundred years. His father called the tree friend; he'd set the seed in the ground. Willard felt the truth of it every Wednesday when he drove to the feed store. Growing up, kids called his father a liar.

They called his father a lot of things.

The grain has no say in how much rain will fall.

"Or how fast the summer flies." A quilt pattern exchange worn smooth over the years. Willard dared a glance in his father's direction, and the breath caught in his throat. Bits of his father's fingers flew away with the wind like thread or goose down, bright, colorful—what was the word?

Iridescent.

For a moment Willard's fear balled its hands into fists and made believe it was anger. He uncurled those trembling fingers and let the feeling go.

So long ago we came, rotations and orbits. His father thought a word that did not survive translation, a shimmering, beautiful knot of meaning. *No longer blank. Colors, so many colors. My heart beats colors; I sing colors. They are part of me now. I tasted the life of this world and knew I could not leave.*

His father's head bobbed like a small gray cloud, the alfalfa flashing hints of green and yellow behind it. As the wind stole him away, the quilts settled lower on the wide seat. The other farmers had never understood his father's ways, said they were alien. Willard hated that word with all the childhood anger of schoolyard knucklebusters. What would those folk say if they could see his father now?

"I can—" Willard cleared his throat of tears he'd never have. "I can pull over if you like."

No. The thought weighed less than a lemon drop breath. *I am glad we finished the planting. When autumn comes, you will need another hand for the harvest.*

Willard nodded, too afraid of words to speak.

When you find that man, look him in the eyes as I have taught you. You will do this.

"I will."

Up ahead, Mel Harvard's blue clapboard truck rattled towards them, an American flag flying from the antennae, wooden crates and rolls of chicken wire piled high in back. As they passed, the other man raised a finger off the wheel and nodded a howdy'do. Willard did the same. He had to. He couldn't do otherwise and not turn around, drive back to the house like the Devil was on his tail and call the doctor. Such a simple gesture, it nearly broke Willard in two.

The trucks parted ways in a cloud of dust thick with summer heat. "It's another five miles to town."

Yes.

"You won't. You won't make it that far."

Near invisible lids flicked up and over invisible eyes. *No.*

Willard chased what he wanted to say a mile up the road. "What should I do then?"

You live. You take me into town, then turn around. The thought faded with his father into the morning sunlight.

Willard took a breath, blinking away dust. He did his best to keep the Ford on the road, his father's memories iridescent in the fields.

Sandra lives in Washington state with her husband, sons, and a grumpy orange cat. She is an avid reader, compulsive writer, and a rabid chocoholic. Her work has appeared in such venues as Jim Baen's UNIVERSE, Daily Science Fiction, Crossed Genres, *and* Galaxy's Edge. *She is a Clarion West 2010 graduate, and an active member of the SFWA. Find out more at writerodell.com.*

THE FISHERMAN'S WIFE

MANNY FRISHBERG

She stood on the cliffside overlooking the sheltered cove where the river merged with the endless water and watched the breakers hurl themselves onto the broad rocks below. The tang of the mist in the air mixed with the salt of her tears.

She was not crying because she missed Eamon, her firstborn, taken by the sea—though she did, achingly—but because she could not join him under the waves. They say only humans cry, but Deirdre knew better.

Walking back home she wrapped her woolen shawl around her to keep out the chill. Her own sealskin coat would have been far warmer—it had kept the cold from her in the frigid Atlantic waters. But it was no longer hers and she promised herself she would not regret that.

There had been a time when she loved that beach. On warm summer afternoons she would come and lay on those rocks, her naked body drinking up the sun, before diving into the water to swim away from the shoreline with her family. Now, there was another family to return to. She had other children who still needed her, and a husband she could finally forgive.

It had been on one such warm, summer day she had first met Jack, a fisherman like most of the men of the small coastal village, like their fathers and grandfathers before them. She had been something to behold, lying there with her long, slender legs crossed so her feet splayed out. She had pale, almost luminescent skin and large, round eyes nearly as black as her hair, now streaked with grey. The rest of her family had already left the beach.

Jack knew right away what she was. He had heard the tales since childhood, the selkie stories his grandfather's friends told around the hearth when the winter winds kept them from rowing out to set their nets. She knew the legends, too—told from the other side—of the seal wives who had to live as humans. How they had bided their time and gained the trust of their fisher-husbands. And how they searched out their skins and returned to the sea, forsaking the families they left on dry land.

She had opened her eyes to the sight of his wind-carved face leaning in toward hers. Before she even reached out to feel around next to her, she knew her gray brindle coat would not be there. He had spotted it as he watched her sleeping and hidden it where he could retrieve it later. She guessed as much from the guilty look on his face.

"Have you seen my coat?" the seal-woman asked, all beguiling innocence. Jack just stared at her, unwilling or unable to speak.

"You have kind eyes," she said. "I can tell you're not a cruel man. You wouldn't keep me from my home and my family." He just continued to stare in silence. Over the years Jack often told folks he believed in love at first sight because it had struck him the moment he saw Deirdre lying on the rock. It always made her cringe.

"Ah, Man!" she pleaded. "Last fall my brother got caught up in one of your nets and he drowned there so the man could take his skin. My mother will die of loneliness if I am lost to her now, as well. Give me my coat so I may go home," she said.

"Neither I nor my father has ever killed one of your kind, nor his Da before that. It was not my net he was caught up in and had it been mine, he'd not have come to any harm.

"But if you're to speak to me, then call me by my name, which everyone knows is Jack. And how should I call you?"

Now it was her turn to remain silent. She knew that he was already in control but she would not reveal her real name, giving him the last bit of power over her. Her stare was neither soft nor plaintive. She had abandoned any illusions about this Jack. Her coat was lost to her until she could find it, and he would do everything in his power to prevent that day from ever coming.

"Very well," he said at length. "I had an Aunt Deirdre, my grandma's eldest sister. She had eyes like yours. If you've no complaints, I'll call you after her." Deirdre nodded solemnly, accepting her new name and, for the time being, her fate.

Day and night she filled his two-room stone cottage with begging and tears and the sailors' laments that had been her lullabies. Her singing was so sorrowfully sweet she sensed that they were tearing Jack in half, wanting to give her what she craved, yet unable to face the dull, grey life he'd lived before her.

After a week Jack finally had to leave her. His crew had grown impatient with his excuses and they all needed the money that would only come at the end of the day with a good catch to take to market.

Deirdre could be patient, and sensible, too. She put aside thoughts of going home, determined to make the life she inhabited now the best she could. Still, when Jack went out to sea and the goats were out to graze, she searched the tiny home for a hidey-hole where he'd hid her skin. After a time she concluded he must have been moving it from place to place, for though she had covered every inch of the house and yard many times over, she never found even a stray hair of it.

Jack O'Dell's strange foreign wife had become a favored topic of the village gossip from the day she arrived and his mates' wives seemed only too happy to look in on Deirdre for him. The village women were properly polite, some even friendly, but they were slow to accept her as one of their own. For her part, she saw little cause for talking early on. She resented their prying gazes and none-too-convincing excuses for "dropping by."

One day, though, she confessed to Gerold O'Keefe's Mary that she had only learned to keep the fire going in the stove by watching Jack make a simple fish chowder after he tired of her serving up what he caught raw. She could not bake so much as a simple loaf of bread.

Mary took charge of her education from then on. Nearly every day she dropped in after the men had gone off to cast their nets. She taught Deirdre by example, sharing the chores to instruct her in how to launder the clothes and cook the simple fare that her husband would want when he came up the hill.

"My Gerold, see, he was a mate to Jack's father before him," Mary said when Deirdre first protested that she was taking up too much of the older woman's time. "And I've known him since he was a garsiúin, as well. We're fond of him and so it pleases me to see he's well cared for. Besides, that old carn of a house can be a lonely place at times." Deirdre nodded knowingly. Loneliness had been foreign to her in the sea, but here it was like a constant shadow over her and she accepted Mary's friendship gratefully.

Mary showed the young wife how to bank the fire in the stove and how to tell when the oven was right for baking bread with the back of her hand. One morning after kneading the dough, Mary related the short tale of her own life while the loaves proofed and they shared a cuppa.

"My Ma had an even dozen children," she said. "I came fifth so I cared for the younger ones, changing nappies near as far back as I can remember.

That's a chore I never minded leaving behind," she said with a chuckle. Deirdre mimicked her laughter, wondering exactly what she meant.

On other days she talked about going to the fair at the county seat, the farthest she'd ever ventured from the house where she was born and of how she'd traded her father's roof for Gerold's.

In Deirdre Mary found a ready ear for any problems she chose to share. If Deirdre was silent about her former life, she talked easily about her current problems. She was genuinely grateful for whatever advice Mary proffered, so after a time the two became the fastest of friends.

"Life here is not so bad," Mary said out of the blue one day, their hands buried in dough. "Not that I know any other. But you come from afar, so you must've seen more of the world than I. Is it marvelous, girl?"

Deirdre stopped kneading. Until then, Mary had always carried the conversation, accepting her silence as shyness, or just her way. She stared at the flour-caked table, searching for something she could say, but what she saw was shell-bedecked spires and waving fields of sea grass. The feel of slipping sand beneath her flippers flooded her mind, filling an aching hole she thought she had buried by now. But she also recalled the scattering schools of herring and only catching a few stragglers. And she remembered the cold fear when the huge, shadow of a whale passed over and her family scattered like herring themselves.

"D'ya ever wander along the shoreline and stop to stare at the creatures caught in the tide pools? Do you think they yearn for the freedom of the open ocean?" she said when her silence weighed too heavily. "I don't. Sure there's wondrous sights wherever you wander but the same sun sets over them all and when it does the western sky outshines them all. And it's friends like you that are the real marvels," Deirdre said firmly. It struck her as she listened to her own words, how far she'd come toward accepting this strange, landlocked life as her own.

Stay anyplace long enough and it starts to feel like home. After that Deirdre began to give herself permission to let herself enjoy things here.

She found herself looking forward to the warm, dark space beneath the duvet and even began to like the feel of Jack's arms draped around her on long cold nights.

Sometimes, in winter, when the sky grew dark too early, they'd light a kerosene lamp and folks would gather in Jack's house with fiddles and drums, pipes and flutes. She'd sit with the wives and children, listening to them sing their songs and tell their tales until the hearth-fire was reduced to ashes. And sometimes, when the tales were of meeting a seal-man on his way to the fair, or they sang of the land beneath the waves, her heart ached with longing but that just made her want to hear them all the more.

Jack never forced himself on her, so when she had been living among the humans for more than two years, Mary ventured to ask how it happened that Deirdre had not begun a family.

"Some of the women say you must be brewing pennyroyal tea," Mary confided. "I've told them you'd never do such a thing to poor Jack. But tell me dear, do think that you're barren? I know a bit of herb lore myself, and there are things you could take that might help." Deirdre had no answer. She stared at her friend, uncomprehending.

"Then did your mother not prepare you for your wedding night?" she said at last and, seeing Deirdre's perplexed look gently explained her marital duty.

So much is strange in this dry world, she thought, but she had her part to keep in the implicit bargain. She had followed him home and bedded down with him since. In time Deirdre even learned to appreciate this Man-Jack's touch and the small favors with which he showered her at every opportunity.

So the seasons slipped by, becoming years as they are wont to, without regard for the daily concerns and long-lost desires for the way things used to be. The day they met grew so distant that even she began to feel as though Deirdre really was her name.

By then they shared a genuine fondness, along with their tiny stone house and five children—four, now Eamon was gone.

Nearly a year had gone by since Eamon had disappeared over the side of his father's fishing boat. By the time they reached his home Jack had turned entirely inward. Silent and taciturn, he allowed his wife to lead him to a chair in front of the hearth while his crew mates told of the disaster in the storm.

"'Twas an evil day from the start, wind, choppy seas, more white caps than blue water," Gerold had told her. "Red skies at dawn, always a bad sign. But the clouds were white like sheared lamb's wool and high, so none of us thought to not go out. But all the morning we watched them colliding with one another, growing flatter and wider, so by mid-afternoon the clouds were a solid gray lid. By then the water had turned grey-green and the waves topped the sides of the boat." He shook his head at young Sean O'Marrough, unable or unwilling to meet Jack's or Deirdre's eyes. When the silence in the little room became unbearable, Sean, a man who usually wore a sly smile and kept his own counsel, took up the telling.

"We hadn't much of a catch to show for all the time we'd spent, but it was past time to drag in the nets before we lost them, and to head back toward land. So that's what we did—we were wrestling them into the boat, sloshing in water up over my feet, so when I heard a splash come on the far side from me, I figured Eamon was baling. But not your Jack. He dropped his hold on the net and raced across the deck like the devil himself was at his heels. Dove straight over the side of the boat after the boy.

"I ran after and saw Jack straining to keep his head above the water, scanning the surface, looking for his son's head to come bobbing up."

Sean had tossed out a rope line while Gerold and the other men worked madly, steering the boat toward Jack before the waves claimed him as well, leaving them to bring the word ashore that father and son had both been lost to the angry sea.

At first he'd fought their efforts to bring him back on board but his muscles were cramping from the cold in the frigid water. Finally, he had allowed himself to be dragged back in like they were landing a codfish.

The whole way back to land, Jack sat shivering in his soaked clothing, wrapped in a glossy black macintosh. Over and over he asked, "Did anyone see Eamon after he went over?" of no one in particular, his eyes set on the receding spot where the tragedy had occurred. "He's a good swimmer," he muttered. "Always took to the water like a fish—a gift from his mother. And he's strong, too, strong as a bull."

Sean was not much older than Eamon. They had laughed together, splashing on the shore before they were old enough to join their fathers on the fishing boats. Now he bore a look of despair so unlike his usual self that it seemed like a mask.

"I never got a sight of Eamon," he told Deirdre, shaking his bowed head. "Not a thing to see but the tail of a great grey seal diving below the surface tumult."

All the while Jack stared into the flames, not seeing how her attention peaked at the mention of the grey seal's dive.

After that, the house felt as grey as the sky on that sad afternoon. But time and the day-to-day demands of keeping the other four children managed to dull the ache and, to her surprise, Deirdre found they actually drew closer.

Out of the blue one night, some months after the tragedy, Jack turned to Deirdre in bed.

"Would you tell me, my dear one, if even now you still long for your old life, the one you'd have had if I'd never come upon you sunning yourself on that rock?"

She lay with her face turned away from him, concentrating on keeping her breath slow and even until he must have thought she had been sleeping and not heard him at all and she had squeezed out the last of her tears. Finally turning over, she took his face between her hands.

"Ah, Man," she said. "You have a kind heart, as I saw that very first day. So I know you have not meant to be cruel. And I do love my family, as any mortal woman might." She smiled at him then but the sadness in her eyes nearly broke his heart, hearing what she left unsaid.

In the morning, as Deirdre watched from the kitchen window, Jack went off on a walk to clear his thoughts. When he disappeared around the side of the little house instead of following one of the well-worn paths, she slipped quietly out the door to see where he had gone. She heard the scrape of the barn door on the rough floorboards and thought perhaps he meant to tend to the goats, though, since she'd learned to do her chores, he'd only done them when she was bedridden.

There were no windows to look through but she could see him through a small chink in the weathered boards. Ignoring the animals, Jack headed straight for a far corner of the barn, where he brushed aside the straw and pried up some splintery floorboards with his bare hands. She heard him curse half under his breath before racing back to the house ahead of him.

Later, when he'd gone for the day, she went to the barn and pulled up the boards herself. But her pelt was not hidden under the floor.

"My life was a lonely one before I came upon you. I may have been selfish but I never had a mind to be cruel," he confessed when she'd put the children to bed that night. "I even imagined that God had put you in my way and you would come to love me as much as I did you."

"I knew the bargain from the first. We have our own tales, you know," she said. "What I could not know is that I might become fond of you. My kind may play under the waves and dance together along the shore but each must catch her own fish. There is no sharing such as your people take for granted."

"The coat was gone when I went to fetch it," he said, the shame in his voice replaced with hopefulness. "But might you have stayed after all, even if it'd been there?"

When the silence had gone on for so long that Jack must have wondered if she was ever going to speak to him again, she said, "Tell me true, Jack, if one day you were swept away at sea and landed far from here, however kind the people, would you not long for home?"

In bed, with Jack snoring beside her, she thought of Eamon and her lost world beneath the sea. Hugging the covers close, Deirdre sobbed softly into her pillow. Then she thought of the daily chores, leavened by Mary's companionable gossip, of Jack and the twins, Brian and Margaret May, who had been so hard to deliver and such easy children to raise. She imagined how Jack would have consoled them walking home from the beach after she'd gone.

———————————

The next full moon was the highest tide of the season. Deirdre insisted that they make a holiday of it. After lunch Jack patrolled the beach of the sheltered cove for the telltale bubbling of rock crabs digging their way into the sand while the children played tag with the incoming surf. She stripped off her clothes to nap on a large, smooth rock at the water's edge.

By the time she awoke Jack and the children had left the beach, letting her have some time alone. The sun was low in the sky, casting a dazzling golden streak across the water, staining the high, sparse clouds brilliant orange, soft lavender and pink.

Deirdre had allowed everyone, even Jack, to think she believed that Eamon was yet another victim of the fickle seas. That was the price the community had paid since time immemorial for the bounty it provided. But Deirdre had been biding her time ever since the morning Jack had found his hiding place empty, making her plans for the night that the selkies would once again converge on land to celebrate.

Around her, naked men and women danced to the rhythms of jangling strings of shells, just as she knew they would. Deirdre scanned the rings of ecstatic dancers, happy to see them. Some faces were familiar yet changed nearly beyond recognition, others too young to recognize at all. Yet none of them was Eamon. It troubled her that she could not pick out her son from among the dancers but she was confident that he'd be there.

Piled on a boulder sat a large pile of sleek, grey and brown pelts, wet and glistening in the bending light. She jumped from her rock and ran toward the pile of discarded seal skins, tearing into it in a desperate search for the one she needed to free herself from her long exile on dry land.

Once she found it she would join the circle to celebrate with them. Abandoning Deirdre for her real self, she'd lift her voice to sing their siren songs and once again dive below the waves.

Then something she saw in the corner of her eye stopped her—it was Eamon, emerging from behind a distant clump of bushes, a pale, brown-haired girl clinging to his arm. They walked together toward the crowd of dancers. At first he stared straight at her without a hint of recognition, then a broad grin replaced the satisfied look on his face.

"Ma," he called out. Deirdre returned his smile, then began pawing frantically through the pile of skins again.

"Ma," he cried out again. Seeing where she stood, the joy in his voice melted into something else, his bright grin turned into a look of dismay.

Eamon broke free from the girl and rushed to his mother, arms outstretched. Deirdre raced to reach her coat before her son could close the distance between them. Suddenly she touched it. A tingle coursed up Deirdre's arm as she pulled the sleek wet fur from the pile, feeling Eamon's hand tugging on her shoulder.

She turned and looked into her son's eyes for the first time in almost a year. Yet she still clutched the skin tightly in her arms, ready to resist any attempt to wrench her longed-for freedom away again. Instead of reaching for the sealskin, Eamon just looked at her, a mix of fear and gratitude, love and desperation on his face.

"I always meant to come back, Ma," he said, his eyes sliding down to the coat she hugged close to her chest. "You remember the lullabies you sang me about the world beneath the waves? When I was just a beag gasur I believed every word of them. As I grew up, I'd hear you sing them to each of the babies in turn and I thought they were just like the tales the old folks tell on a cold night.

"Then, one night I woke up late to hear Da going outside. So I followed to see what on earth he was doing. It was pitch dark in the barn but I could hear his scraping around in a far corner.

"I stayed out of sight and, when I figured he was safe and sound back in bed, I crept in to see for myself what he'd been up to. That was when I found the skin. I didn't know right away what it was but the night was bone-chilling cold and I'd been standing about with nothing but my bedclothes on. I wrapped the pelt around myself, just to get warm and all of a sudden my legs were gone. I found myself flat on the ground, flapping around like fish." He laughed and Deirdre's breath caught in her chest—it had been so long since she'd heard his laughter.

"Scared me half to death," Eamon went on. "I pulled it off as quick as I could and buried it again, just like Da'd left it. Then I ran back to my own bed. But I didn't sleep a wink the rest of the night.

"I couldn't shake what had happened to me from my mind. A few days later I dug it up again and hid it under some gear in the corner of the boat. When the storm came up, I saw my chance had come. I put it on again and dove into the water. I was going swim right to shore and bring it back, I swear. I only wanted one look at the world of your songs, just once to see those palaces of coral and pearls from the lullabies.

"But once under the waves it was so hard to even recall that I'd ever had a life on land or to think about the family there that'd be missing me."

Staring into his eyes, his mother gave him a sad smile. *How well I know,* she thought. *It's not hard to believe at all.*

Over his shoulder she could see the young woman that had come from behind the rocks with Eamon bathed in golden moonlight. She stood out of the way but close enough to hear every word. Deirdre could see the softness in the girl's gaze when she looked at Eamon and the look of dread when her eyes met Deirdre's. She did not utter a sound but that look spoke volumes. Deirdre looked at her son once more and let the mottled sealskin fall at her feet.

"I do know," she whispered, more to herself than to Eamon and walked off to the side of the rock to gather up her clothes.

She stayed for a while on the beach as the moon turned pale white and climbed the sky. She danced among her old friends, adding her voice to old songs she had not sung for years.

When they donned their coats again and sidled back into the waves, she put on her human clothes and walked alone up the steep pathway to her home and family on the hill.

At the top of the cliff, overlooking the place where the river merged with the endless water, she stopped and watched the breakers hurl themselves onto the broad rocks below. The tang of the mist mixed with the salt of her tears. She was not crying because she missed Eamon, her firstborn lost to the sea, but because she could not join him under the waves.

They say only humans can love their children more than life itself, but Deirdre knew better.

Manny Frishberg has been making up stories since he started staring out windows. He spent the first half of his life learning what to write about and the second half learning how. He is spending the third half of his life writing them, inflicting the results on an unsuspecting public since 2010, along with a lifetime's worth of news articles and feature stories. A freelance editor, he lives with his wife near Seattle, Washington.

LAKE THIEVES

CHRIS KURIATA

Following a map drawn on the back of a bloody cocktail napkin, Dad raced our family station wagon across the winding dirt roads of Pelham. My brother and I broiled in the sweaty backseat, begging for the air conditioner. Dad stepped on the gas, kicking up thick clouds of dust we watched turn orange in the punishing sun, making the back of the car look like it was on fire.

Dad pulled off the main road. We drove through farmland, beneath an old ranch gate, before parking out front of a peeling, red barn. The farmer sat in the shade of the open door, cradling a gas powered chainsaw. I imagined him firing the blade up and carving his initials in our car door, sparks flying everywhere.

"My sons are on the roof," the farmer warned, gesturing over his shoulder. "They got scope rifles and they'll fire at first sign of funny business."

Smiling friendlier than a crooked Bible salesman, Dad stepped out of the car and stretched. He cracked his back, making a POP POP POP sound and going "Ahhh," like he'd just had a refreshing guzzle of soda pop. After the trip we'd endured, my brother Josh and I would have confessed to anything for a cold soda pop.

With his hands on his hips, Dad surveyed the land, giving a respectful nod to the sights we knew would soon be familiar on every farm in the country, maybe the world; the quaint house smothered by boarded up windows, the still smouldering heap of the burned down chicken coop, the acres of brown crops abandoned to drought...

I craned my neck, peering through the windshield at the top of the barn, not believing the old farmer really had sons up there—sons he claimed were Navy Seal crack shots. Josh grabbed my shirt and pulled me away from the windshield, afraid I'd get shot right between the eyes. I told him to relax, the farmer was lying. That old phoney knew his rusty chainsaw threatened no one (the gas tank probably wasn't even full), so he only pretended to have sons watching over him.

"I got money for you," Dad said, pulling out a thick wad of bills.

Josh poked a finger into my ribs and pointed inside the barn.

"Keep quiet," I said. "I can see them too."

Inside the dark hayloft, mammoth figures hung from the highest rafter. Pale bones reassembled in the shape of cows and bulls dangled in mid-air like museum exhibits. Such an installation must have taken months to construct. I knew bones didn't snap together like plastic pieces in a model kit. All those skeletons had to be wired together; from the heavy, horn adorned skulls, to the little bones spiralling over the hooves. Seeing these naked, double and triple-headed animals defying gravity changed my mind and convinced me of sons on the roof. Someone had to help the old coot hoist those monstrosities up there.

Dad slapped every last dollar into the farmer's hand, looking glad to be rid of them. He had put ads in the newspaper, inviting shoppers from as far as Etobicoke to take advantage of his fabulous deals. His customers scooped up our pool table and lawn mower, as well as the snow blower, and the computer from Dad's office. He allowed a woozy-looking woman from Thorold to rummage through the closet, selling Mom's dresses for a buck apiece. Mom wasn't happy about that.

"This stuff is junk," Dad argued. He fanned the stack of bills in Mom's face. "When the time comes, you're gonna be glad to have a little extra dough instead of some dress you haven't worn in years."

Mom rolled her eyes and said, "If you think when the time comes that money is going to be worth anything you've got pudding between the ears."

The farmer stuffed the money into his overalls. Dad handed the napkin with the directions to the farmer, who squinted at it from all angles, like an antique dealer authenticating a treasure map. Once satisfied with its legitimacy, he took an old fountain pen and drew a new road onto the map.

"Now in case anyone takes this map away from you, I drawn it in reverse. When the road goes right you go left, understand?"

Dad understood. As we drove into the forest, I watched the barn recede, keeping an eye peeled for the farmer's sons. I thought I spotted them on the south slope. I tried waving but they did not move. Bolder, I gave them the finger. No reaction. They slouched like they had been propped up there years ago, their bones wired together same as the hanging bovine.

"Why did he do that?" Josh asked.

"Protection," Dad said. "Some people believe suspended bones will frighten off unwelcome visitors. Or it's a sign of respect, inviting strangers and offering your subservience. I forget which."

We followed the farmer's map, turning left when his oily drawing turned right. Josh kept quiet, but I could tell by the way he repeatedly rubbed his eyes he was trying not to cry. It finally sunk in we weren't going back for Mom. When we passed the final gas station an hour back, Mom begged Dad to stop so she could use the washroom. "I want to pee like a civilized person one last time."

Dad regretted the decision before he'd even finished pulling in. Nervous, he drummed his fingers over the steering column while Mom hustled between the pumps to ask the attendant for the bathroom key. While we waited, Dad punched the radio buttons, jumping across the dial like he was looking for a special message being broadcast just for us.

"What the hell's taking so long?" It had barely been a minute. "I don't think that woman is with us 100%. I think someone filled her head with a different way to survive. The wrong way."

The windows of the gas station were cluttered with cigarette and lotto signs making it impossible to see inside. Dad backed up a couple of feet, and we caught Mom leaning across the counter, either trying to kiss the attendant or whisper something in his ear. Was she flirting or begging him for the phone to tattle on us?

Dad punched the gas, making a *ding-ding* as we rolled over the belt, leaving Mom and the station behind. "Screw it," he said. "We're cutting our losses here."

Josh looked horrified. He pulled off his seat belt and pressed his hands against the back window. I told him Dad was just making a mean joke. When he cooled off, we'd turn back and find Mom sitting in the shade of the pumps—cold bottles of soda lined up at her feet, waiting for her thirsty boys to return.

I no longer believe Mom waited a single minute for us. I think the moment we left, she thanked whatever god she still believed in and took off running in the opposite direction, anxious to get back to the city, where she believed she could adapt to the coming changes just fine without us.

Selling our belongings bought us directions to a forgotten cabin on the lake, hazy through the swarm of buzzing black flies. Dad loaded the top of the car with fishing poles and tackle boxes, making sure we had hundreds of special lures to choose from.

"It's time we did some fishing, men."

We found a motorboat tied to the rickety dock. Dad stuck a reed into the gas tank but it came out bone dry. We heard it scratch the bottom of the hollow tank.

"That cheating son-of-a-bitch," Dad said. He snapped the reed and looked around, as if for management to complain to. His anger only lasted a moment before he clapped his hands and threw the big grin back on his face. This was going to be fun. "We need to get on the lake. Time's a wasting."

Dad siphoned gas out of the car and soon the three of us bounced across the water, rods in our lap. Josh and I could barely cast with the bulky life jackets restricting our arms, so Dad made us pull them off and dump them in the water.

"There is a change coming," Dad said as our lines cut across the smooth glass of the lake. "People have been whispering about it, passing along things heard and things dreamt. It's like a giant game of telephone when you don't know even half of what's true."

I'd noticed the whispering. In the supermarket, a man standing in the fruit aisle gauging a melon's ripeness would be approached by a stranger who cupped their hand to his ear and whispered something delicate. I saw it happen on the street all the time. People stopping one another. Whispering. I don't know what secret they poured into one another's ears, but the receiver often looked terrified or wept tears of gratitude.

"There's too many voices out there," Dad said, trying to stay hush, not wanting to scare the fish. "But if you're smart, you know which ones to listen to. You're not going to save yourself hanging bones overhead or burning down your house and covering your skin with ashes or whatever foolishness your mother believes. You know any day now the news is going to start telling people to dig shelters in their backyard? All bullshit."

Josh gasped. Dad had never cursed in front of us but we were men now, deserving of grown up language. When we got back to the car, Dad would probably dig into the cooler and share a beer to seal our manhood.

Dad tapped the side of his head, grinning like a mad genius. "The fish in this lake, that's the key to surviving the transition." He opened the tackle box, dressing our lines with the biggest, wildest lures certain to land us a life preserving catch. "Why do you think this water is tucked so far away where nobody can find it?"

The fish in this lake were special. That's what Dad sifted out of all the whispered warnings. Anyone who wanted to survive better get their hands on a fish and fast, there were only a few of them out there.

Fishing is about waiting, enjoying the passing of minutes and hours without scratching the itch of boredom. You forget how to read your watch and start gauging the passage of time the way nature does, by the movement of the sun or the erosion of rocks along the water's bottom.

But Dad enjoyed none of these time delicacies. Afraid our success depended on choosing the right feathered lure, he didn't give us long to troll through the water. Every ten minutes he'd cut our lines, tie on a new hook and have us recast.

Josh pulled up a small sun perch but Dad yanked it off the hook and tossed the crushed, bloody body back into the water, saying it was too small, not the fish we were looking for.

"How do we know when we've caught the right fish?"

"Oh, we'll know."

We fished all day, Dad unrelenting with his knife, cutting the line and abandoning our hooks over and over. We let hundreds sink into the green murk beneath the waving reeds. At some immeasurable distance in the future, the lake would dry up leaving nothing but a bed of cracked mud and a mysterious collection of fuzzy, multi-coloured flies for the stars to puzzle over. *Now where do you suppose all those came from?* they'd ask—humankind's presence on the planet too small of a blip to even register on their memory.

Our arms began to grow sore.

By nightfall, we had yet to catch a fish. Once the sun lowered into the lake, you couldn't see an inch beneath its thick, black surface. I felt like we were floating on miles of oil. One dropped match and the whole shebang would burn for a millennium.

Dad fiddled with our rods, nearly yanking them out of our hands. "You guys have to stop fooling around and catch a fish." The way he rubbed his eyes, I knew he was trying not to cry. Dad second guessed himself, worried he'd made a mistake, listened to the wrong whispers. Maybe the fish in the lake weren't the key to survival. Maybe the man who sold him the map and had cheated him. The transition was coming and we were doomed like everyone else.

The smile returned when a small light appeared on the other side of the lake. His optimism soared at the promise of other fishermen. Dad pulled the engine cord and we sped towards the bobbing white speck. We didn't even have time to reel in our lines.

"Don't say anything," Dad instructed us. "Just look mean."

At the sound of our approaching motor, the other boat switched off their light, hoping to drift invisible. Escape by paddle was impossible; they could only sit in the water, hoping we'd pass by exchanging nothing more than a friendly wave.

"Look real mean," Dad repeated.

Cradled inside the second boat was a man with two young girls, nearly the same age as Josh and me. The man looked bulky and muscular, making Dad seem withered, like someone stunted by childhood disease. The new man looked like he could flex his muscles and rip his shirt just like the Incredible Hulk.

Despite his physical advantage, the man was frightened. He understood his muscles were no match for the desperation on Dad's face.

"How you guys doing this evening?" Dad asked, gripping the rim of the other boat, keeping us floating in tandem. "Catch anything?"

One of the girl's eyes involuntarily flicked to the cooler on the floor of the boat.

"Give us a look. Let's see what you caught."

The man considered his options. Conceding defeat, he opened the cooler and gave Dad a peek at the fish his daughters had hauled out of the lake.

"Oh, that's a nice one."

There was life in the fish. He flapped his tail in a puddle of thick slime, a disgusting mix of lake water and blood trickling from the hole through his gums. The fish didn't look very special to me. I expected the skin to be translucent, allowing us to see the marvels of its incandescent circulatory system, his glowing blood lighting up the lake like an emergency flare.

"What did you use to catch him?" Dad asked. One of the girls held up her rod, a bare, plain hook dangling from the end.

The fish flapped its tail, getting agitated. Its mouth flapped open, giving me a good look at its thick teeth—two rows of square enamel choppers, thick as a horse. No doubt he could bite off your finger.

"We don't got any guns," Dad said. "We have no unfair advantage over you. Each of us has the exact same tools to fight with—whatever nature gave us."

"I don't want to fight-"

"Shut up. Now, a big muscle-head like you probably thinks he can take me. But remember, I got my two boys here. While you're struggling with me they're grabbing your daughters and pulling them to the bottom of this lake. My boys can hold their breath underwater for three minutes. Been training 'em since they was small. How long can your daughters hold their breath? One minute? A minute and a half? We can find out, or you can give us the fish and get lost."

Without hesitation, the man handed over the cooler. Dad tried not to smirk but he couldn't help himself. He felt proud in front of his two sons, Hey, your old man showed that gorilla a thing or two.

Motoring back to the cabin, Dad said, "See, they had it coming. When they caught their fish they should have packed it in and headed for shore but they got greedy and stayed out to catch another. Fine, let 'em catch another fish. This one's ours." Above our heads, the stars began to wink out, as if someone with inky fingers were blotting the night sky. We crossed the lake blind, knowing we'd reached shore only when we crashed into it.

The cabin had no electricity so Dad shone the car headlights through the front window. His nervous hands struggled to open the cooler and dump the fish onto the table. Outside, the air filled with a hollow whooshing. It sounded like a giant sea shell planted in the sky, moaning so loud we'd all go deaf.

The fish continued having life in it. He flopped his tail, looking around the cabin with large cow eyes. I was taken aback when the fish blinked and I realized it had feminine eyelashes. The fish waggled his fins and stretched his mouth open wide. The damn thing was preening and trying to smile, showing off as many white teeth as possible. The fish wanted to show us he had personality. It wanted to be our friend.

A chill ran down my spine when the fish began singing. A fish's throat runs all the way down their body, allowing them to develop a deep and melodious voice. There were no words of course, fish can't speak, but he sang an uplifting tune that borrowed from birds and the serenity of wind blowing over reeds. It was a song I had heard before but forgotten until this moment. I wasn't sure if it came from a dream or someone on the street whispered it into my ear. In a state of reverie, I reached for the fish, wanting to stroke him, certain his scales would tickle my fingers like feathers.

Dad brought the hammer down on the fish's bright, white smile. The teeth shattered like walnut shells and broken pieces flew across the table. Dad turned the hammer over and used the claw end to pry out any remaining shards. Only when the gums were naked did Dad risk touching the fish, using his thumb to fold down the sharp top fin and begin hacking off the head. He worked fast and soon the tail stopped flapping.

He cleaned the fish roughly, as though he had never done so before, only ever seeing a diagram of the procedure. He slit the belly and folded the fish open like a newspaper, the tough outer skin cracking.

"This looks delicious. Who wants the first piece?"

Dad offered a hunk of pink flesh off the end of his knife. White bones poked out and a few glittery scales winked at me in the beam of the headlights. I picked the fish off the blade and stuffed it in my mouth. It didn't taste special, just soggy like undercooked eggs. The taste made me wince. Clearly a bottom feeder.

We ate the fish down to nothing, leaving only the tail, head, spine and scales sitting in a pile of broken teeth. Dad urged Josh and me to eat, serving us three pieces to every one of his.

"Eat up, men," he said. "This is special nourishment. This will give you the strength to survive the transition."

The sound of boots stomped across the porch. The cabin door opened and the muscular man Dad stole our fish from entered. He looked sad, like he didn't want to be here. Dad pulled me and Josh close to him. The muscular man didn't have his daughters; he had traded them for three men following him into the cabin. The men carried rifles, the first real guns I had ever seen in my life. I knew they were also going to be the first I ever heard fire.

Dad held up his hands, nodding as if to say, Okay, you got me. He respected the fisherman for playing fair, bringing three men; one for Dad, Josh and me each. At first, I thought the fisherman had met the rifle men in the woods and called upon their sympathy to help right the wrong done to him, but by the way the men pushed him around I soon understood the nature of their relationship. The men with guns had waited at the fisherman's camp on the other side of the lake, expecting him to return with the special fish. When he came back empty handed, they said, "Bring us to whoever took it."

"I'm sorry," the fisherman said, looking genuinely remorseful. "I had to tell them what happened. I didn't think we'd find you." He glanced back at the car headlights blaring into the cabin, an enormous pointing finger announcing WE ARE HERE.

I wondered what happened to the fisherman's daughters. Had they returned to camp on the other side of the lake? Likely, there were more men with guns keeping an eye on them. That worried me. Men with guns bored easily. There was no telling what they would do to those girls.

Having no desire to witness what was coming next, the fisherman left the cabin. The men with guns didn't notice him go, they kept their sights on us and the table of fish remains. I thought the fisherman would take the car for his troubles but the headlights continued shining into the cabin long after he left. I hoped the men back at camp on the other side of the lake would show mercy and shoot him the moment he appeared on the horizon, never letting him get close enough to see what they had done to his beautiful daughters.

Dad inched himself forward until he stood between me and Josh and the men with guns. Dad watched them stare at the fish remains and he knew what they were thinking.

"I had the lion's share," Dad lied. "I was greedy and afraid and I fed myself before my children. What's in their bellies won't be worth the effort to retrieve."

The men lifted Dad and slammed him onto the cleaning table. Dad didn't smile and put on a little dance like the fish in an attempt to endear himself. He didn't want the men picking up the hammer and bashing his teeth out. He needed his teeth to clench when the real pain started. The men wouldn't waste a bullet euthanizing him before retrieving their precious fish.

I trust Dad did his best to save us, but some nights, when Josh and I shiver in the backseat of the station wagon, I wonder if he offered himself up to the men with guns in order to escape living in this new world. Maybe he listened to the hollow whooshing in the sky and thought about the disappearance of the stars and decided surviving the transition wasn't necessarily the best one could hope for.

The headlights died ages ago. Josh and I live out of the car, enduring this new existence, too dark to tell where the lake ends and the sky begins. So dark we might as well be blind. The persistent drone in the sky has killed our hearing. The ground vibrates constantly, as if something is stampeding towards us. Josh and I shiver and hold each other, failing to sleep, wanting to ask one another (but never daring) who did Dad really save sacrificing himself like that—us or himself?

Slowly, things are changing. The horizon has begun to distinguish itself, turning a barely perceptible shade lighter, like a cup of coffee with a single drop of cream mixed in. Over time, the light will expand, as surely as the rocks continue to erode. Soon enough, we will find our way to the crashed boat and cross the lake, on the off-chance the fisherman's daughters are still out there, shivering tight in one another's arms in a tree hollow, barely surviving, just like us.

Often, Josh and I feel our way into the cabin and run our fingers over Dad's tough remains. We feel his mouth of clenched teeth and the smile along his stomach where the fish was retrieved. We leave the cabin door open and smash all the windows to encourage bugs to find him and nibble him down to his bones. Using fishing line, we'll stitch his skeleton together and hang him from the trees just like the bulls in the old farmer's barn.

We don't know if Dad's floating skeleton will serve as a warning or a welcome for whoever is coming, but as the horizon continues to brighten and the tremble in the ground grows to an intensity that nearly knocks us over, I guess we'll find out soon enough.

Chris Kuriata lives in the Niagara Region. As well as editing documentaries about murderers, faith healers, and hockey, his short fiction has appeared in Taddle Creek, The New Quarterly, *and the Exile anthology* The Playground of Lost Toys.

TEARING THE HOOD

GERRI LEEN

Red. Red is for blood. Red is for death. So many ways the story can go.

Like this. Grandmother gave me a red cloak. I wore it proudly, until a bad man saw me and wanted me and took me.

No. Not a man. A wolf. That's it. A wolf. Because lone wolves who take the place of grandmothers are common.

My, what big teeth you have.

No. Wait. That's not right.

You see, I know wolves. They are shy, skittish creatures that hide from humans. They live in packs of family groups, and they howl at the moon—that howl is often all you hear of them. Wolves don't invade homes.

My, what big eyes you have.

Wolves don't pretend to be what they aren't.

My, what big ears you have.

Wolves don't play guessing games.

Humans do.

No one wants to hear how it happened. You do? All right. I can tell this in a more straightforward way.

Perhaps you could unchain me?

No?

It's a sad story. I tell it better when I can use my hands. Truly.

You don't trust me. How can I trust you with my story—with my truth—if you won't reciprocate?

Fine, at least turn up the light. It's so dark in here.

The better to see you with.

Grandmother took me in when the villagers rescued me—their words, not mine—from the wolves. The pack became my home when my parents were murdered on the road and their belongings stolen. I got away. My mother told me to run far and fast, and I did.

I ran even farther and faster with the pack. As a wolf sister, I played with the pups and was treated like the other youngsters. I was six when the wolves found me; I was fourteen when the villagers took me away from them.

Their pelts hang on the walls of the town hall. The villagers thought the pack killed my parents. And I had no words to tell them the truth, not after eight years speaking wolf.

I couldn't say it wasn't a beast that butchered my parents, but a man. I didn't know to protect my pack.

I didn't know how quickly a howl could be silenced.

The better to hear you with.

Grandmother took me in—actually, Grandmother locked me in. Wooden floors under my feet, the sky hidden away by walls and ceilings. I howled for a week before I finally understood that my old life was gone.

I bit her. Poor old woman. She lost her only son and then to have me thrust upon her? I heard her crying more than once.

In the pack, when a member was troubled, we nuzzled. We rolled and tumbled and cajoled the member out of the funk.

I was bigger than Grandmother. I didn't know how strong I was. I was only trying to make her happy.

The better to hold you with.

She broke her hip when she fell. It's why she was in bed when *he* came looking for me.

I never saw his face. I was running, far and fast, and I never saw his face. He could tell that I didn't remember him. He saw that I was...pretty.

Pretty and wise to the ways of the forest. He was a woodsman. That would be useful to him. In a wife.

Grandmother was glad to see me go. I had hurt her, and she didn't understand that I never meant it to be that way.

He smelled bad, and he had eyes like those of the male badgers drunk on mating. The pack steered clear of them during their ruts.

Why did I stay with him? You think I didn't run? I did. He called me back with the yelp of a wolf pup—one of my pack mates, somehow saved when the rest of the pack was killed. I heard my little brother cry out his terror and loneliness.

I went back. He put the pup down, put a rope around his neck, the end of it tied to his belt. I followed him to his house, shivering as I tried to comfort the pup.

Did I wear the red cloak when Grandmother gave me to him? No, it was my mother's. It was in her trunks, in the wagon, taken by the woodsman when he killed her and my father.

A fact I realized when I entered my new home. I recognized their things. The faint smell of my mother lingered on this cloak, the odor of my father on the fine leather slippers that were too small for the woodsman but sat in his closet anyway, like trophies.

They were not the only shoes in the closet. The smells of those other owners were unfamiliar but varied.

In the pack, bad behavior is dealt with in prescribed ways. But a crime such as this—murder—wasn't known. I had to make my own punishment.

The villagers think I turned on him, a savage creature, the same way they think the pack killed my parents.

I wasn't frenzied when I did it; his axe worked as well in my hand as it ever did in his.

The better to kill you with.

I tried to show them the shoes. I tried to get them to smell them.

They killed the wolf pup. They hate wolves and they hate me.

And that's why I am chained here, Magistrate. That's why they want to hang me. I stopped a killer. He would have killed the pup once he started to grow; he would have killed me the same way he hacked my parents to death.

There are no shoes in his closet? Only his boots?

The villagers must have stolen them. They were, as I said, fine shoes.

Are you sure you couldn't unchain me? I really can tell this story so much better with my hands.

Gerri Leen lives in Northern Virginia and originally hails from Seattle. She has stories and poems published by: Daily Science Fiction, Escape Pod, Grimdark, *and others. Her first solo editing gig, the* A Quiet Shelter There *anthology published by Hadley Rille Books, was released in Fall 2015 and benefits homeless animals. See more at http://www.gerrileen.com.*

WHEN AN ANGEL MOLTS

H.L. FULLERTON

We keep the angel in the basement. It's my job to collect the feathers. Some Mother sells, others she uses in her magics; I'm not allowed to keep any. I'm not allowed to leave the house either, unless Mother takes me. I think she's afraid I'll tell someone about the angel and they'll take him away. Or maybe she's afraid I won't come back and she'll have to train a new drudge. You can never be sure with Mother.

She doesn't share her secrets. Mother says, "Secrets are like diamonds. You have to mine for them and when you find them, you keep them or sell them, but you never give them away. Especially not to ungrateful daughters who don't finish their chores." Mother is a very good miner. She can even unearth my thoughts. That's how she found me when I ran away.

After she dragged me home, Mother made my leash. She tethers me to the iron ring above my bedboard. When it's chore time, she takes the lead off and I just wear my collar. The angel has a leash, too, but his is more shackle and chain. He never gets to leave his room.

Neither of us is going anywhere. Mother binds the things she likes best.

———————

At first sight, I thought Mother had captured the sky. Or stolen it. The angel's body was cloud white with veins of gray; his wings, shades of blue. Then I saw his face. Cheeks like glaciers, pupil-less eyes flash blue then gray like tiny storm clouds, a sharp, hooked nose more beak than human, and below, two angry slashes of blood red lip.

Mother pushed me into the cell and said, "Bring me feathers."

The angel screeched as I stumbled about the room, snatching fallen feathers from the floor. And still I found it hard to take my gaze from his. Even angry, he was the most beautiful thing I've ever seen.

I crouched and ducked beneath flapping wings, like when I harvest priests' fingers in bat-filled catacombs—Mother always sends me into the darkness first because I am her eyes and ears.

"To your right," Mother called and I turned in that direction. Whack! The angel's wing caught me. Bones cracked and I fell. The angel lunged, trying to tear my face, but its chain was too short. I crawled to the door and begged for Mother to let me out.

Mother said, "You dropped some feathers." She wouldn't open the door until I recollected them. She was mad because she heard my angel-thoughts. Before today, she was the most beautiful thing in my world. "Still think it pretty?" she said, taking the feathers from me. "Next time it will be your neck."

I am better at feather-collecting now.

The day the angel lets me pet him, I almost cry. His feathers are so soft, so *soft*. I brush my fingers over them, catching the loose ones and tucking them away for Mother.

I can't believe he's allowing my touch. I keep glancing at his face, but he keeps his eyes averted. My hands shake. The more I try to steady them, the more they tremble. His wing moves beneath my touch.

"Does it hurt?" I ask. Even my voice shakes.

He cocks his head and stares at me. His eyes like faceted gems, beautiful and hard.

"I'll stop if it does."

The angel turns his head and acts like I don't exist. He reminds me so much of Mother then.

I don't know if angels can talk. Ours doesn't. Sometimes I dream of growing wings and flying into the sun. I never make it. Even in dreams, Mother's leash pulls me back. And I am careful not to think too loud about leaving—Mother might be listening.

Once I asked Mother if angels eat and she slapped me. "It isn't a pet," she said and I didn't get food that night. I worry our angel will starve. He's been here three, maybe four, months. His feathers aren't as shiny; his eyes are filmy; he doesn't flap and screech as much. He no longer smells like fog and ozone. If the angel dies, I will be alone again with Mother. I will miss the silky press of feathers against my skin. The way his vanes tickle. The soft wispiness of his tightly-curled down. The jerky tilt of his head and his quizzical eyes, so blue and deep.

Mother is in her stillroom, making potions. Soon it will be time to collect the feathers. I shadow my thoughts, cloaking them to hide my secrets. I stare out my window at the sky and think TIRED. (Picture the angel soaring in the clouds, disappearing into blueness. His coloration would make him near invisible.) The sun pricks my eyes and they water. I think of the heat of the sun on my (his) face.

I sit up suddenly, think of the dust on the stairs I must sweep. The clothes in the hamper that need cleaning. I wonder if there is enough soap (I bet the angel misses the sun's light) to wash them. (Spell jars.) We are low on furniture polish; I should make more. (My collar feels tight.) I head downstairs to the kitchen and begin washing dishes. I dry the plates, the cups, the spell jars and put them away. (One large jar finds its way into my pocket. I hardly notice it.) I sweep the stairs and make furniture polish. I wash the clothes. THERE IS ENOUGH SOAP. I take my clean aprons to my room. I put them away (Open my window.) I straighten the quilt on my bed (stick the uncapped jar out into the light). I hum (catch the sun in my jar) while I work. MUST GET FEATHERS SOON.

I hear Mother at the bottom of the stairs, calling me. TIME FOR THE ANGEL. I (quickly screw the cap on the jar, trapping the fresh air inside, shut the window, hurry) hurry down into the basement.

When I'm sure Mother isn't looking, I pull out the jar—it squirms in my hands like a living thing—and hold it towards the angel. He shifts away, but I shush him and step closer. "For you," I whisper and uncap the jar.

His nose twitches, he leans closer to the jar, sniffing. My magic worked. I can see the rays shining from the glass, bathing his face. He closes his eyes and basks. Too soon, it's all gone. "I'll bring more when I can."

I think, maybe, angels drink sunlight.

Yesterday Mother searched my room and smashed all the spell jars I'd hidden. She leashed me to the ring above my bed, muttering incantations and curses the whole time.

"Think I don't know about your feeding the angel? I know *everything* you think."

(Except Mother is a liar. She doesn't know about my feather.) I cried because that is what Mother wanted. "I had to feed him," I blubbered. "If he dies, we won't have any more feathers. Please, please let me go." I had to beg all night, but by morning she freed me to clean the house. And to collect the feathers.

I am lucky angels hate the smell of demons or Mother would have traded me to them again as my punishment. People sometimes come to see Mother when they think demons are tormenting them. These people are fools. Demons may be invisible, but they are foul-smelling, nattering things. If a demon is in bed with you, you know it. Good thing Mother covets feathers more than demon spunk.

I will miss the angel when I go. Since Mother is with a customer, I don't have to be as careful with my thoughts. She's too busy making magic to worry about me, and I've been very good (ever since I found the feather) lately.

When Mother finishes with her customer (next goes to market), I will (escape) pluck three long feathers from the angel's hide to keep her happy. Mother doesn't like that the angel is shedding less and less. She stares at him and purses her mouth and shakes her head real slow like—Mother is deciding what to do with his body.

It makes me sad.

He doesn't flinch when I yank out Mother's feathers, but it must hurt. I pulled three hairs from my head and that stung. And his quills are so much thicker. He doesn't bleed, which annoys Mother. She says she can do great things with angel blood, if only he would shed some. I cut myself with Mother's athame and willed myself not to bleed, but my veins didn't listen. Mother got angry about the mess.

Well, that's what she said, but I could tell she was more mad about not knowing that's what I intended to do. Mother hasn't realized that her thought-mining is starting to work both ways.

I dream of dead angels and it heartens Mother.

My feather. I hadn't planned to steal one, but when I undressed and found a pin feather nestled between my breasts, I tamped down that spark of hope like Mother extinguishing the flame in a fire moth's eyes. I thought about the blisters on my hands (while my fingers caught the tiny, curled wisp) and how tired I was (how easily it will slice through Mother's magics).

I picked at the puffed skin on my thumb (pricked it with the tiny shaft) until it oozed (and hid it in my pillow amongst the goose feathers). Then I curled up (like a feather, like a feather) and rested my head on its softness.

I felt it shift beneath my cheek, settling into the down, secreting itself, and (forget, forget) forgot about it.

"Go on," Mother says. "Say goodbye to the angel. I know you want to."

I stare at my porridge and fill my head with thoughts of sky-bright wings and cloud-colored skin. Once cumulous white, his skin is now rainy day gray. I picture him decomposing, (flying free, sunlight caressing his face) wings spread, bald patches showing scaly skin.

Mother laughs. "You can't hide from me."

I think, *I love him more than you*, and fight not to smile when her lips tighten.

I am an ungrateful daughter—her thought or mine, I'm not sure.

As I open the angel's cell, I am smiling. Until I think of the coming goodbye. Will he understand? He never responds to my words, only rarely acknowledging my touch, but then I am his captor. I WILL MISS HIM WHEN HE'S (I'm) GONE. I open the door and shriek.

He is tearing mouthfuls of feathers from his already ravaged wings and spitting them on the floor. A pile big enough to stuff a pillow covers his feet. His eyes, more alien than usual, glow with feverish light.

I rush in and try to stop him, pull his head away. "Your wings," I say. "Your beautiful wings. Stop, stop, please."

He shakes me free, his madness giving him strength, and continues plucking.

Mother pulls me from the room, a cloud of feathers enveloping us both. She makes me strip to ensure she gets every last feather.

I laugh because she is too late, too late, and my screeching echoes the angel shredding himself to pieces.

"I suppose I will have to sell it sooner than I expected," Mother says, shooing me out of her stillroom. "I don't suppose you got any of its blood on you?"

But no, it's all my own.

Mother is going to Gackles to find someone willing to buy an angel. I think (Today is the day.) disappointing thoughts as she chains me to my wall.

"It's your fault," she says, still angry about the angel eating its feathers. They made her magics potent and now she will have to use inferior substitutes. "You spoiled it. You're lucky I don't sell you as well." An idle threat; Mother has no intention of losing me. Her thoughts are so clear now.

"No!" I say because she expects it and I don't want to raise her suspicions. Gackles is the furthest Mother ever goes from home. She took me there once—before I ran away and she brought me back. Gackles is on the cusp of decency, where dark and light mingle. Angels patrol not a block away. It takes twenty minutes to get there. That's how long I have to escape. Maybe, when I'm amongst decent folk, I'll confess about the angel and they'll come and free him. But most likely, Mother will have disposed of him by then and they'll blame me for his disappearance.

"I thought if he liked you, he would bleed for you. But now...when I get back from Gackles, the demons can have you."

Mother smiles at me and leaves. I keep my mind blank. Then I fear that will be suspicious and picture terrifying things. Her mind tugs at mine. I feel her energy move down the street. (Twenty minutes, twenty minutes.)

I think of my pillow (the hidden feather) and worry (what if I can't get the feather to work?) about what will happen to the angel (me).

Mother is almost at Gackles. Her delight sizzles into my brain; she expects to make a good deal on the angel. My fingers—I pay them no mind—worm their way into the goose down and sort through the feathers, feeling for a particular softness. (Found it.)

I open my palm and, keeping my thoughts quiet, look at my treasure. It is smaller than I remember and I don't have to feign disappointment. I only have one chance. If I mess this up, Mother will ensure I never get another.

Maybe I shouldn't go.

Holding that thought in my head, I saw through the ring with the angel's pin feather. Both my collar and leash are spelled; breaking either will alert Mother. So will leaving the house. I must time these perfectly or she will catch me before I reach the light lands.

The feather is sharp, but the ring is thick. My fingers are bloody from pinching the tiny shaft. I make the final cut and the feather's shaft splits in two.

I slip my leash from the ring and dash down the stairs. The broken feather clutched in my hand will make messy work of the collar. Trying to get it off, I may very well slice my own throat. But if I leave the collar on, Mother will use it to track me.

I feel a tingling at the back of my neck: *Mother*. She's coming back. She knows something's wrong.

At our home's threshold, I pause. I could leave wearing the collar, cut as I run. If Mother guesses my route, it makes little difference whether I remove the collar now or before I reach the light. We both know where I'm headed. Whoever is faster wins. But Mother has magics to call upon to aid her speed that I do not. Despite my planning, I've already failed. Unless...

I steal another feather, a stronger feather. If the angel has any left. *The angel...*

I never said goodbye. I hurry down the basement steps and fling open the cell door. He is featherless. My eyes scan the room and it too is clean of feathers. I sob and Angel lifts his head from his chest.

Those blue gem eyes wound me.

Dots of blood appear on his hide, like pin pricks. He is bleeding for me.

My hands clench into fists and his last feather stabs my palm. If I leave him to Mother, I'm as bad as her. Worse, maybe—because I know what he'll suffer in my stead.

"Can you run?" I say.

Angel looks at me, head cocked.

I rush to his leg chain and begin sawing. "You have five minutes. Turn left when you leave the house."

I can't tell if he understands me. I picture my route in my head and hope he can mine my thoughts. His chain is thicker than my ring. Time is being eaten up.

"Run three blocks, then turn right." Mother is coming.

"Fly, if you can." His wings, his poor wings. They'll never work.

"Go one more block and turn left. You should be able find help there." I can't feel my fingers any more. I'm bleeding all over him.

"You need to be fast. She's coming back and if she catches you, it'll be worse. Much worse. Do you understand?"

He jerks and the chain snaps. Something pops, black flashes streak about the room. A spell. Mother bespelled his chain. "Go!" I scream. "Go!"

I pull at him, uncertain if he can support himself after so long in captivity. He is heavy and nearly topples us. I heave him up the stairs. His legs start to work, but not soon enough, I fear. Mother is running. She is close. Six blocks away. I can hear her chanting in my head.

The angel flings open the front door and I shove him through. Gloomy sunlight coats his skin. How much worse he looks in the light of day. I hold in my mind the image from when I first saw him. He was magnificent then. Now on the patchy lawn in front of our wicked house, he looks three-quarters dead.

"Call your friends if you can."

He doesn't move.

"Run." I make shooing motions with my hands. Blood flicks over him. "She's almost here. You have to leave."

The collar at my neck starts to burn. One of us will be free, I tell myself, and what do I know of freedom, I've only ever dreamt of it. He can't live without it—and Mother won't be able to track him. If only he'd leave.

He beckons me to join him. "I can't come with you. She'll find me. She always finds me."

He spreads his wings and lifts his head to the heavens. My vision blurs; I collapse against the doorframe.

"Fly," I whisper. "Fly." But without feathers, he can't.

Then: his skin changes color. No, his feathers grow back. Shades of blue and white, patches of dove gray. More beautiful than ever. His summer eyes lock with mine and he shoots up into the sky like a reverse lightning bolt.

I follow his flight until the sun blinds me and Mother blindsides me. Her fists are so angry, she will make me pay in blood and pain, but I lock the image of my angel, wings spread, rising into heavens, in my mind and nothing can break through it. Not even Mother, no matter how hard she tries.

Through swollen lids, I imagine my angel standing, wings folded, in front of me. I wish I told you how sorry I am.

You just did, his image says.

For real, I wish I could apologize for real. I close my eyes one last time. I hear the rustle of feathers and feel air rushing past my skin. I pretend I am raised into the bright light of the heavens. I turn my head and welcome the night.

Mother always sends me first into the darkness—I am her eyes and ears. But this time I'll search for patches of gray and eyes of blue and clouds like a summer's day.

H.L. Fullerton writes fiction—mostly speculative, occasionally about angels— which is sometimes published in places like AE, Daily Science Fiction, Writers of the Future, Vol. 32, *and Parsec's* Triangulation *anthologies (*Last Contact *&* Lost Voices*).*

A Clown's Quest

Gunnar De Winter

Applause.

The sound waves of synchronized claps pulsate through the Clown's virtheatre.

"Ladies and gentlemen, allow me to welcome you to my humble virtual stage."

Standing in the middle of a large spherical cage with an algaplast skeleton, the tall spindly man spreads his long arms, folds one before his stomach and arches the other one into the small of his back while he bows. The many miniscule compound lens cameras, modeled after the eyes of dragonflies, broadcast every move and sound to his spectators in exquisite detail. 3D straight to the retina.

Thousands of viewers are looking at a rendition of a large stage, heavy red velvet curtains pulled back, with a bright spot capturing the Clown in its beam.

"I can almost taste your search algorithms, sifting through the datanet, trying to grasp my nature, trying to see whether or not I'm a fraud whose claims exceed his capacities."

The pale Clown, clad in an ancient chalk stripe suit, taps his large nose twice. His gangly virtual appearance mirrors his real look, but plenty of subtle alterations ensure that he won't be recognized easily when he ventures out in public, rare as that may be.

"Correct, am I not?"

The trousers and sleeves of the suit are about two inches too short, exposing thin, bony limbs, adding to his unconventional guise. A carefully crafted persona.

"Whether it's your first time, or you're one of my highly valued returning fans, please cease your data-queries, good viewers. After all, I present you with the only first-hand source of the particular information you seek." His thin eyebrows dart up and down as he leans forward, bringing his hawkish face closer to a few cameras. "Me. For your convenience, for your growth, I shall bare my heart and soul to you. Tomorrow, same time. See you then." An exaggerated wink.

He taps a button with his foot—encased in a shiny black-and-white dress shoe—and ends the transmission.

For your convenience. And my salvation.

He checks the number of hits.

31,026. *Good.* That should get him sufficient credits to prepare for the second act. And to acquire news on data-queries of his own. He refuses to believe he is the only one left. There have to be others. And he will find them.

He wipes his performance smile from his flexible face and glumly changes into the bland grey overalls that have become commonplace. It's best not to stand out when he leaves his apartment on the 271st floor of one of the cloud-piercing skyscrapers that occupy most of the city's available land. Actually, the spires are cities in themselves. You could live your entire live in one without ever having to leave, an increasingly popular way of life. Efficiency is key.

He mindlessly navigates the narrow corridors, divided into two lanes by short fluorescent stripes. Up on the habitation levels only pedestrian traffic is allowed. The transparent wall in the distance tells him he's nearing the edge of the inner cylinder. A small line is waiting as the glass elevators slide past with impressive speed.

With slumped shoulders and slightly bent knees he stares down.

Blend in. Don't stand out.

If anyone would suspect his true nature, he'd be hunted, probably ending up as some rich person's exclusive emotional emitter. Not a prospect he relished.

A blurry green in the distance is the only sign of the parks. Somewhat higher he notices the busy scrambling of ant-sized people on large and seemingly floating platforms occupying parts of the meticulously calibrated inside atmosphere.

"Next." The emotionless voice wakes him from his daydreams.

He gets in the glass cage. "225, please." The doors close and the elevator drops precipitously, causing him to grab the railing.

"225." The doors slide open without a sound. He exits and follows a path he knows all too well.

He stops in front of an inconspicuous door that's neatly integrated in the wall. 225.016b. He fights the urge to knock. The door disappears sideways. A short woman nods at him, her dreadlocks braided together in an ornate structure on top of her head. Snakes frozen in mid-air.

"0.nyx," the Clown slightly inclines his head.

The ebony woman lifts a tailored eyebrow. The Clown recognizes the gesture and enters the apartment. Shelves line each wall, stuffed with various information storage devices and data-sifters. The modern equivalent of a bibliophile's lair.

"Need a refill already?"

He nods.

"Shows are going well then?"

He shrugs. "Can't complain. You've got it?"

"Of course." She rummages through the technological artifacts on a shelf and conjures up a jar filled with a clear viscous fluid.

He frowns. 0.nyx had retrieved the recipe from who knows where and guarded it fervently, so he depended on her if he wanted to keep performing. *Knowledge is power.*

0.nyx motions her client to the metallic full-body chair with black padding that claims a central position in her flat.

The Clown sighs and walks over to it. He sits down and unzips the top of his overall, exposing a skinny pale torso, veins and ribs vying for visual supremacy. All for show. He accepts the scalpel 0.nyx hands him. With clenched jaws, he makes a small incision below his left armpit. The index finger of his right hand enters the cut. He exhales. There it is, the socket. She hands him the cable. He inserts it as she places the black VR immersion helmet on his head.

Time for payment.

The images, carefully selected by 0.nyx from across many archives, assault him, violently pulling the emotions out of him. Unlike his regular audience that craves just the most salient feelings, 0.nyx is painstakingly assembling a full library of emotional experience. She tries to hide it, but the Clown notices. Joy and desperation follow in rapid sequence. Physical and neurological responses are carefully recorded, encoded and sent through the cable ("wireless is never safe," she always reminds him), pouring into the dock behind her right ear. From there, the data travels onward to the secure cache integrated with her brain stem.

Quickly fluttering eyelids indicate that 0.nyx is receiving her client's feelings. Raw and unadulterated.

The visual battering ends, leaving the Clown panting. A lifetime of emotions in less than a minute. With a frown, he looks at 0.nyx, whose eyelids are slowing down. Mimic. But a good one, though. She'll quickly pull apart the data strands and add them to her already impressive database. She'll learn to emulate the emotions, thanks to target-specific neurotrophics perhaps even to the level of her neural pathways. But it still wouldn't be her feelings. His frown deepens. *Would they?*

"Satisfied?" he asks.

Her gaze reasserts its focus. "You've kept your end of the bargain. As usual."

"Your turn."

She hands him the jar.

"Anything else?" he enquires, unable to completely ward the taint of childish hope from his voice.

0.nyx' dreads sway gently as she shakes her head. "No. The first-hand emotion codes I've been analyzing can all be traced back to a single source: you."

He swallows, his prominent Adam's apple bobbing like a piece of driftwood.

"See you next time," she says, bluntly ending his visit.

His mind wanders during the return to his small flat.

He's one of the few that remain. One of the final androids, the machines that live and breathe. That think and feel. Once, there were a lot more of them. But, as steep as their increase was, so abrupt was their decline. Soon after the first generation, humans and technology merged. The novelty of man-and-metal blends quickly wore out. Androids were rendered superfluous before they even realized what they were. Most couldn't handle it and shut themselves off. Permanently and irreversibly.

By now, almost all humans had become integrated with technology as much (or even more) than he was. But the differences were inescapable. Vat-grown vs. naturally conceived (granted, often with carefully selected gametes, but still). Tailored to feel vs. upgraded to analyze.

An android with feelings stuck in a world of emotionally stunted humans. The sad irony haunts him like a predator that stalks its prey without striking, without pouncing to deliver the redeeming *coup de grâce*. But the true predators were the humans, eagerly gorging on the emotions they extracted from him. So he had learned to bait them, to give them the shame and pain they seemed attracted to. He catered to his audience and gave them what they yearned for.

He blinks. He's back in his flat. Experience-based subroutine algorithms have led him here while his higher cognitive functions were preoccupied with existential worries.

A sigh softly pierces the oppressive silence. He's tired. Exhausted. Time to recharge. Literally.

He lies down on the body-mold mattress and grabs the cable springing forth from the large plastic bag containing energy-producing algal sludge. He swallows the business end and, with his tongue, guides it to the palatal plug hidden behind his uvula.

Tomorrow: Act two.

He opens his eyelids, which seem to get heavier each day. He pulls the cable out of his mouth and massages his hollow cheeks.

Time to prepare.

He changes into his stage costume, which isn't really necessary, but, somehow, helps him maintain character.

Hidden in a corner of his living room stands an antique dentists' chair. Superfluous now, just as he is. All over the world, engineered bacteria guard mouths vigorously, molding teeth in perfect symmetry along the way. He drags it into the camera-cage and rolls a small table of implements to its side.

He slumps into the chair and think-commands his bionic lens to open his private inbox. 0 messages. As usual. Then, he navigates to the most heavily protected area in his personal data ocean. Bits and bytes come at him in an unceasing torrent. Data aplenty. To no avail so far. It's all his. No sign of others. He shuts off his lens.

With a sudden move, he cracks his skinny neck. It's later than he expected. Recharging is taking him longer and longer.

Anyway, show time.

He flips the switch and activates the cameras. He stands up and forces a smile.

"Ladies and gentlemen, welcome back. As always, a pleasure to see you. Or rather, to have you," two index fingers point forward, "see me," two thumbs point back.

His audience once again sees a large wooden-floored stage. This time with a shiny metal chair in the middle. He spreads his arms and turns on his heels. Walking around the chair, hand tracing its outline, he continues.

"I know, I know, you're impatient. So, let me get down to business. I'll deliver what you want. In return, do transfer the agreed amount of credits, please. Those who don't, will be excluded from further viewing." *And pay no attention to the tiny virtual viruses that hitchhike along with your quarry, insatiable emo-vampires.* The tiny passengers that travel with his emotional outpourings to his clients will soon start their own surreptitious task, unseen and unheard. Except by him, of course.

He shrugs sheepishly. "A man's gotta eat. Even if he is just a clown."

"And yes, you might think you can get your hands on my product another way. But I doubt it," he pokes a long finger at the cameras and his eyebrows crawl up to the edge of his bald scalp, "because there's nothing like experiencing it first-hand, which is why my audience tends to guard what they gain here vigorously from others, as all of you will undoubtedly do too." He leans back and spreads his arms again. "Besides, it's a small price I'm asking for. In fact, my accountant declares me mad."

No laughter. No one ever laughs. The silent moment passes.

"Alright then. Get ready."

He slips out of his jacket, tosses it aside and begins to unbutton his grey shirt, exposing his chest. The veins and ribs form an intricate map, leading to a treasure. A treasure he's about to unearth. Three thick red welts are all that remain from the previous show.

He places himself in the chair.

"Ladies and gentlemen, I give you... my heart."

The Clown, still smiling, grabs a scalpel from the small table and places it beneath his collarbone, on the beginning of the first welt. He breathes deeply and pushes. Blood wells up. The scalpel moves towards his other collarbone. The only signs of discomfort are ever-so-slight facial muscle tremors. He doesn't turn off his pain network, but keeps his nociceptors blaring. He wants to—needs to—feel this. He proceeds with an identical cut just above his diaphragm. Both cuts are connected by a third that neatly divides his upper torso into two identical mirror images.

Briskly, he puts the scalpel away. It clangs on the table. There's blood, but not that much. The human semblance only runs skin-deep, he thinks wryly.

Handling his own body as carefully as an old, leather-bound tome, he folds back the two skin flaps, revealing the ribbed bioplast casing underneath. Through the foggy colorless shell hints of his innards are visible. A dark fluid flows and a few bright green lights shine like stars piercing through a cloudy night sky. The gasps from the audience exist only in his mind.

Unintentionally, he swallows and fights back pain-induced tears.

"Indeed," he says, forcing cheerfulness. "This is how androids tend to look on the inside. But I'm sure you all have seen my kind, whether it's in person—which would be a rare occurrence—or through some 3D rendering. However, I'm also sure that you've never received a direct link to our inner world, to an android's soul."

After these deliberately lofty words he grabs a small cable and pushes it through a soft, barely visible sphincter in the casing, a bit below his left collarbone. He guides the slithering data-snake to its destination.

The cable plugs into his upper heart data-dock and he stifles a moan, all the while maintaining his on-stage smile. His emotions pour out, neatly translated into bits. His pain and humiliation. His longing and loneliness. He only has to think about his quixotic quest to conjure up the feelings his audience seems so drawn to. All converted into convenient data packages, they're sent to his spectators for greedy analysis and solitary study. Wildly, the data streams into the great invisible data ocean that engulfs the planet.

Well, into an encrypted portion of it.

His feelings weren't free. And the true price was hidden from his clientele.

That's enough. Panting, he unplugs the cable. "Enjoy, dear viewers. I'll see you tomorrow for the wrap-up." He taps his foot on the off-button and the second act of his show comes to an abrupt ending.

His smile vanishes rapidly. He tilts his head back and closes his eyes. For a while, he just lies there, in his old dentist's chair. Then, he gets up carefully and walks over to 0.nyx' jar on a small table tucked away against the outer wall of his living room. He folds the skin flaps back into their proper place and smears generous amounts of the smudge over the cuts, which gluttonously slurp it up as they already begin to close and form thick red welts.

The Clown shuffles back to the performance chair and falls into it. He sighs and closes his eyes again. Act two always leaves him exhausted.

TING.

The sudden sound startles him. An emergency message. On his personal encrypted account. It could be only one person. 0.nyx.

He activates his lens. The message is exactly four letters long.

NEWS

Could it be? He gets up and hurries out of his flat. Swiftly he walks through the parts of the skyscraper where most of his life plays out until he nears flat 225.016b.

Anticipating his arrival, the doors slide open before he comes to a full stop. Not waiting to be invited in this time, he marches straight through.

The onyx woman is standing in front of the outer wall which has been turned to its transparent setting. She's staring out at the smog that obscures most of the neighboring skyscrapers.

"Well?"

0.nyx turns around and lifts an eyebrow when she sees his strange attire. He ignores it and taps his right foot to spur her on.

The eyebrow descends. "I might have found something."

"Go on."

"I found a few bits of raw emotion code I can't tie to your broadcasts."

He feels a smile tug at the corners of his mouth. A genuine one for once. "Does this mean that...?"

With unaffected voice 0.nyx responds. "There are a couple of options. The most likely one is indeed what I assume you've been hoping for: another android. It could also be a human being who's been able to successfully emulate a full emotion equivalent, or was born with the skill. Or, it might just be an anomalous piece of code."

"Yes, yes," he nods vigorously. "Where?"

"If my inferences are correct: one of the 605.223's."

"What? Here?"

"Yes. Not that surprising really, even with the global data availability, the scrapers tend to form clearly distinct nodes in the worldnet."

He shakes his head. "Then why did it take so long?" Too long.

"There are only a few of your kind left. And most of them spend their lives anxiously trying to blend in, to keep themselves hidden in plain sight. They're not as resourceful with their emotions as you are."

He still has a hard time believing it. He's trembling. "Okay, I'm going up there. You keep looking and let me know the moment you've got a precise location."

She nods.

Just before he leaves, he turns around. "0.nyx?"

"Yes?"

"Thank you."

Hesitantly, she smiles and nods. "You're welcome. Part of our deal."

For a brief moment, the Clown wonders whether that was a real smile or just an emulation from her vast library of socially acceptable emotional displays. But the excitement of the moment drives those thoughts quickly to the background. Alone no longer. It echoes through his mind.

He's lucky. It's lunch time, so there aren't too many people around. The elevator arrives swiftly. He gets in and directs the glass cage upwards. As the transparent transport rises, he takes a few deep breaths. Another android, hiding on the higher levels, where luxury and decadence are as vital as food and shelter. Would it be a servant, or one who has successfully blended in with its erstwhile creators? *Doesn't matter.*

"605," the androgynous elevator voice tells him.

The doors slide open and reveal a large hallway plastered with thick red velvet. At least it looks like velvet, but he knows it's an algal mat recycling carbon dioxide and other waste products, exuding fresh oxygen and mild stimulants. At these levels, the pleasure center in your brain is constantly tickled.

Already beginning to feel giddy, the Clown marches through the opulent corridors with spritely steps.

TING.

0.nyx again.

605.223c-d.

He smiles and turns right brusquely. There's no one in these luxurious hallways. Rumors are that the inhabitants of the high-level habitats have their own private elevators, leading them to wherever they want without having to mingle with others.

Aha. He has arrived. Following his gentle knock, a sphincter opens above the large and intricately engraved wooden door. Real wood, a sign of extreme wealth these days. A camera-eye on a fleshy stalk emerges. With a sudden move, it retracts. Another squishy sphincter opens at chest-height on the left side of the broad door.

INSERT ARM. The command appears in the red velvet when the swaying strands rearrange themselves.

He does as he's told. A sting. He winces, but manages to keep his arm in place. The machine's looking for DNA. He grins. *That's going to be a surprise.* The DNA of his organic parts clearly shows signs of purposeful manufacturing.

He hears a gentle buzzing, as if the probe hesitates, unsure of what it has found.

Unexpectedly, the door opens and the stinger retracts, spraying heal-fast on his skin. Surprised, he looks around and enters.

"Hello?" Slowly, he traverses the lavish lobby made up out of various intersecting planes of smooth material in different degrees of shading and transparency. It's as if he's walking through a glass cathedral. Suddenly, he becomes painfully aware of his attire. Knowing that it won't help, he still reflexively pulls his too-short sleeves.

"Hello?"

He leaves the lobby and enters a more traditionally luxurious living room. Clean, expensive furniture everywhere. *Is that real leather?* Everything's smooth, and white and red. As he reaches the open door on the far right, he notices an unmade king-size bed. Shiny chrome bedposts support a pile of pillows and blankets. From underneath the duvet mountain, a foot peeks out. Female. Pale.

Carefully, he inches closer. "Hello?" No movement. He scrapes his throat and repeats more forcefully. "Hello!?" Still nothing.

Standing before the heap of bedcovers, he decides to peel them away one by one. Soon, long blond hairs appear, followed by an attractive young face. A pale face with livid lips. A face without life.

No no no.

Brusquely, he puts a large, skeletal hand on her neck. No pulse. His breathing speeds up.

"No no no," he mutters, giving voice to his earlier thoughts. He flings away more blankets until there's only one left. His hands trace the outline of her face. He opens her mouth and puts two fingers in. *Please, let this be a mistake. Don't be...* But there it is, the palatal plug. Exactly like his. Struck by the electricity of realization, he jerks back his fingers.

His neck loses all tension and, as he sits down, his head flops forward in despondency. He buries it in his hands and sits there for a while, unmoving. A statue of sorrow.

Finally, reluctantly, he drags himself through the molasses of stupor and, with profound disregard for the physical integrity of his skin layer, smashes the surface of the nearest glass table. He selects a shard of the right proportions and sharpness. He walks back to the bed, removes the final sheet, turns the body, and puts the tip of his improvised knife beneath the left breast.

"Sorry," he whispers. The glass sinks into the flesh smoothly. Until it hits the hard bioplast casing. With a pained expression, he pushes his eyes closed. After a deep breath, he opens them again and cuts away three edges of a square. He folds back a small portion of the female android's flesh cover, exposing her heart.

There is no more light. The darkness inside her tells the sad tale of her permanent departure.

He slumps on the bed, carelessly discarding the stained glass shard.

"Why?" He looks at her as if he's expecting an answer. "I... I'm here. I'm here. I heard you." *But too late.*

The first signal from one of his kin he ever managed to pick up turned out to be an emotional suicide note.

_____

He wakes up the next morning, unable to remember how he made it back to his apartment. He can only hope he adequately covered his tracks. Not that it would matter. Her android nature would be blatantly obvious, and she would become a study object rather than a victim.

Don't give up. He repeats it like a mantra, hoping it will motivate him enough to get through another day.

There must be others, hidden among these emotional vampires. Even he broadcasts using a fake persona. Perhaps one day he'll find another trace and won't come too late, won't arrive after the solitude resulted into a final outburst of code before the eternal dark.

Perhaps.

He gets up and drags the chair out of the camera cage. Time for the final act.

With a tap of the foot, he switches on the live-feed.

His audience trickles in, seeing him standing on the large stage staring at the wooden planks under his feet.

With an almost inaudible sigh, he conjures up the trademark smile.

"Welcome." Something is missing from his voice, as if dash of vitality has been drained from it. "I trust you enjoyed yesterday's show? I also trust you've hidden away the data in your deepest and most protected virtual vaults. Knowledge is power after all." He winks. As he goes through the motions, thanking them for watching, urging them to return and bring their friends, he continues his monologue internally.

And by making you open up your vaults, I snuck in a custom-made piece of code, exploiting your data-caches for any and all information that can help me in my search. Fools. Do you really think I give a shit about your personal development, about your credits and childish desire for my emotional pain? I've infected your precious data with a virus you'll never even notice that combs through your painstakingly assembled code from behind all the levels of fancy encryption you've installed so carefully, so confidently.

His speeches, both from mouth and mind, come to a close.

"And so, I perform. Until the lights…" The background darkens.

Even if I have to infect the whole world and corrupt every piece of data,…

"Go…" The Clown inclines his head as the final glimmer of light leaves and the curtains close.

I will find the others.
"Out."
Applause.

Gunnar De Winter is a biologist/philosopher who occasionally performs fictional fieldwork.

On Rising One Snowy Evening

Karen Bovenmyer

The first thing I saw when I clawed my way up through the frozen earth was Vaughn's tractor, drifted with four inches fresh snowfall, glimmering in bright starlight. In the yard beyond, the farmhouse was dark. Were all my kin asleep? Gone this time? I pulled myself the rest of the way out of the ground, leaving behind a grave full of broken earth shaped like a milkweed pod. My boots punched through a stiff layer of ice over more snow under the fresh dusting. They'd buried me in cowboy boots this time, not knowing what season I'd come up. It didn't matter that the leather was thin and crackled with ice. I didn't feel the cold, and my bare hands weren't even chapped from the dig.

Not ready to face the house just yet, I tried to gauge how much time had passed by Vaughn's tractor. I touched the rear tire, smearing my palm with black—too many years—the rubber was breaking down. The door opened with a screech of binding metal, the cab thick with rust. I climbed up and sat down on the cracked seat, fingered Ishtar's sun-faded eight-pointed-star talisman I'd hung from the rear-view, and took a deep breath. Under the smell of old mouse nests and rotting leather I still smelled Vaughn's tobacco, and I closed my eyes to the powerful memories of summer sun, bailing hay, and water slopping down his muscled arms as he drank from the bucket I brought fresh from the well. My husband, gone before his time, leaving six kids half-orphaned and 160 acres to till.

I fingered the eight-point talisman and repeated the vow I had made (was it seventy years ago? Eighty now? I'd have to ask my youngest up at the house to be sure). The vow that I would never leave our children, for death or nobody. I had them bury me here each time, by the rusting tractor, so when I came back I would remember my vow to the Sumarian Ishtar, goddess of my immigrant Iranian grandmother, who returned me again and again from her sister, Ereskeigal, Queen of the Dead, when my family had need of me.

I opened the door, my boots found the big step down, and I made my way across the yard to the house. Someone had painted it since last time, and the sloping porch had been repaired. It wasn't easy watching the big old farmhouse Vaughn and I had built with our own two hands fall into disrepair over the years. I always liked waking up in years like this one, when times were good and it was in good repair.

I didn't ring the doorbell, just let myself in and left my boots on the rack. My socks had rotted, but the denim of my jeans and canvas of my coat were still good, and I picked my way across the living room barefoot. It was a prosperous time indeed—gleaming glass and metal on the wall in the living room, a device that sent images and sound long distances, much larger and thinner than before. A new rug under my rocking chair. The kitchen counters replaced with marble. The pantry full. I looked at the photos on the new refrigerator—a graduation announcement for my great-great grandson. A whole new crop of babies growing up through elementary—the big family of my youngest daughter had grown. Ten years, must have been, since I'd been here last.

But why had Ishtar wakened me? All looked more than well. I crept slowly up the stairs, careful that the creak of wood might wake a child too young to have met me and learned the family secret. I passed memories on my way down the hall, of lean years feeding my six kids as I passed their bedrooms, and the many returns meeting their kids and kids' kids until the only flesh of my flesh remaining was my youngest, baby Mary, whose cheeks had still been round when I made the vow.

Her bedroom door was open six inches, just like she always liked it, a rectangle of golden light shining through it. I opened the door silently and let myself in, whispering her name, the sound rough in my unused throat. She was propped on my big brass bed, one of the quilts I had made her draped over her thin knees. She'd fallen asleep with a book across her withered lap and, despite the thin grey hair she'd gathered into braids, and the wrinkled, wizened face of an old woman, I saw my child, my baby Mary, asleep under a dog-eared copy of *The Long Winter* by Laura Ingalls Wilder.

I moved the book aside and settled down on the bed next to her, my cold hands finding her bent and knobby ones. Her breath was shallow, but her watery eyes opened. I felt a spike of fear in my chest. I thought I knew now why Ishtar had sent me this time.

"Mary, it's momma. I'm here."

"Mom." Mary sighed, her voice tremoring with the quaver of the very old. "You look just the same." Her eyes scanned my face, then dropped to our hands—the reverse contrast of young and old. "It's my time, isn't it?"

Fear took my voice, but I nodded, because just then I knew it was true.

"You kept your vow. All these years. What will happen to you now?"

"I don't know," I said, and I sat with my youngest child as she breathed her last. She weighed almost the same as she had when I made the vow, and I found it no more difficult now to lift her in the quilt then when I'd first made it. I took the eight-point star from Vaughn's tractor and lay back down in my grave, pulling Mary close, the talisman between us.

When I next woke, it was to golden sunshine and the scent of fresh-mown hay and tobacco.

Karen Bovenmyer earned her MFA in Creative Writing: Popular Fiction from the University of Southern Maine's Stonecoast program in Summer of 2013. She is lucky to train future faculty at Iowa State University, where she works primarily with aspiring Ph.D. students who enthusiastically share speculative-story-idea-generating research.

TABU

LISA LEPOVETSKY

What a coincidence, meeting you here at the cottage, Heidi. The moon's beautiful on McKellar Lake, isn't it? Hard to believe how cold and deep that water can be, even on the hottest, steamiest day of summer. But I guess the prisoners old Nathan Bedford Forrest threw in there back in the thirties found out. He claimed they drowned trying to escape his prison camp, but there have always been those other rumors floating around. He probably didn't do it himself, but most of those prisoners were black, and some of his guards weren't exactly fans of the Civil Rights movement, if you know what I mean. And Nathan Forrest was more than willing to look the other way. No, you're right. That's not stuff we learned in civics class.

From what I've been told by people who go scuba diving down there, some of the stones at the bottom still have parts of skeletons tied to them. And they say the spirits of those poor souls don't rest easy. But, of course, I've never been able to find out for myself, not with this mangled foot. Some prisons don't have walls.

No, don't go; this could be a chance for us to get to know each other better. I'm just working on a jigsaw puzzle. Come on, you can sit out here with me on the screened porch and watch for... whoever you're meeting. Jigsaw puzzles have a way of bringing people closer, filling in the gaps. You can help me work on it.

Here's another piece with a flat edge. It must go on the border—although sometimes they fool you, sometimes things aren't exactly what they seem. I've always loved this puzzle. Remember the picture? It's from those old advertisements for the perfume Tabu, with the violinist holding the pianist draped over his arm, kissing her. I feel—I don't know, all tingly inside when I look at it. Just imagining her, limp in his arms like that, while he still grips the violin in his other hand—it gives me the shivers. God, the passion he must feel for her. And that hint of danger in his eyes—I like that, too. Like Terence Stamp and Samantha Eggar in The Collector.

You haven't? Oh, I love old movies. I could watch that one over and over and never get tired of it. He plays this butterfly collector who's obsessed with a college girl and kidnaps her because he loves her so much. It must be exciting to have someone love you so passionately they'd be willing to do anything.

Well, no, I suppose she wasn't exactly willing, but that's not the point. Or maybe it's precisely the point. Violence, pain doesn't matter, it only lasts for a moment. What matters is the passion. That kind of passion is everything, and it lasts forever, longer than people or photographs or even the darkest mud under the Mississippi. Like hate—the hatred of slaves for their masters, or prisoners for their keepers. You can still feel it in the air around here, even though they've all been dead and rotting for more than a century. Sometimes I see things...

Or here, take a good look at the picture on the box lid there, for instance. Her right fingertips still dangle against the piano keys. It's because he dragged her up right in the middle of a song. Imagine the passion he felt, the pain. What do you suppose she's playing? "The Moonlight Sonata"? "Prelude to the Afternoon of a Faun"? It should be something by Debussy, but the picture is called "The Kreutzer Sonata," so that's probably it. They're classical pieces. No, that's not really your style, is it?

Of course it matters what she's playing. The whole image is so powerful, so scary, all it needs is the music to make it complete. And the fear, of course. Just looking at it, I get goosebumps, don't you?

Oh. Well, different people respond to different things. I learned that a long time ago. Like Mother always says, one man's poison is another man's meat. Or is it, one man's poison in another man's meat? No matter.

Here, Heidi, This one looks like it must be his hair. See, it fits right in there. James's hair is like that, all stiff and wiry, kind of like the underbrush out there by the dock... James Woodridge. You must know James. He works at the same company as your father; he's in the mailroom. Handsome, tall, very ambitious.... Yes, that's right, that James Woodridge. I knew you knew him. Who wouldn't notice him—all that thick black hair that makes you wonder what his chest must look like, and the rest of him... I've heard his father worked for Nathan Forrest and his mother is descended from Chicksaw Indians. Isn't that romantic? I understand Chicksaw squaws had ways of treating enemies that made even their braves cringe. But that's another story.

A crush, on James? I think it's more than that. Much more, actually. Don't look so shocked, we're both nearly adults. I know you've been around. You're probably the most popular girl in the junior class. I guess you'd call my relationship with James a love affair.

It is true. I wouldn't make that up. He came here to the lake with our family almost every weekend these past few months. Daddy hired him to do odd jobs for the summer, mostly repair work. Nobody's used this building since it was part of Nathan Forrest's land, and it was a real mess when we got it—overgrown with weeds and even bees building honeycombs in the walls. Sometimes I lick the boards, trying to taste the sweetness.

Of course, there haven't been any prisoners to use for slave labor here in a long time, so Daddy had to bring in an outsider. There was plenty of hot, sweaty work to build a man's muscles during long summer afternoons.

And now summer's over. School starts next week, and nobody'll be coming down here anymore. You can almost smell that sense of things ending. And you should feel that water. It's cold as death out there tonight.

But James never minded; he just jumped right in anytime. He liked to explore the bottom—said he was going to bring me back a bone from one of the convicts. But he never did. James was like a member of the family—in most ways but one. I guess what happened was inevitable. If Daddy wasn't out in the woods hunting with his rifle, he and Mother would take the canoe and go fishing during the day. Of course, I couldn't go, since I'm not allowed to swim. But, while the cats were away, we two mice would play. Nothing serious, you know, but those few quick kisses opened up a whole new world for me.

Here's a black and white piece, it goes in the piano somewhere... I suppose at sixteen most girls are still just messing around in the backseat behind the football stadium with some pimply football jock, deciding how far to go. You probably know how that is better than anyone, being a cheerleader and all. But things have always happened differently with me.

You know, Heidi, you're my only friend. Stop stammering, you don't need to be embarrassed; I know I'm not really your friend. No, it's all right. I'd guess you're a little embarrassed to be here with me tonight, aren't you? You're glad there's nobody else around to see.

Mother and Daddy are down in Memphis tonight, at dinner and an art show opening at the gallery; they left this afternoon. James told them before they left that he'd take me to Mud Island for the day. Lies. Lies have always come so easily to him. And, of course, Mother and Daddy wanted to believe him, so they did. They would never imagine a young stud like James finding anything appealing about me, not with this ruined foot. Wouldn't they be surprised?

I suspect Mother was relieved to think I didn't want to go to the opening with them; she tries to pretend she doesn't even notice my foot, but I can tell I embarrass her. She had an affair before I was born, and thinks I'm her punishment. I don't even think she loved the man, just used him to hurt Daddy. People use other people all the time. Look at this picture—he's about to use her—or is she using him? Anyway, I never blamed Mother—not for that, anyway.

No, I'm not sick, just a little chilly. I keep shivering, can't seem to warm up tonight. Probably the dampness from the lake; I'm surprised you're not cold. But thanks for asking. Almost like a friend would.

You know, I've never had many friends. No close ones. You know how kids are about abnormalities, especially the ones you can see. Sometimes I could hear the other kids whisper "hopalong" or "gimp" behind my back. And then they'd giggle. Those giggles were the worst. I can't stand hearing anybody giggle. It's such a nasty, biting little noise—like gnats. James' laugh is deeper, like a rumble of thunder across the hills. I shudder just thinking about it.

You know, one of Nathan Forrest's prisoners had a wife and daughter who worked at Nathan's house. The mother was a cook and the little girl helped her. She was only twelve or so at the time, and she had a clubfoot, too. Isn't that a coincidence? The story goes that one of the guards got drunk one night and raped the little girl. To cover up his crime, he threw her into McKeller Lake. She drowned, of course; couldn't swim with a clubfoot. They say any prisoners who died on the property were thrown into the lake, and maybe some who weren't quite dead. But those are just gossip.

No, that piece is part of her hair, not his. See how it twists there like a noose? It goes in the center of her bun. If you turn it the other way, I think it'll work. Here, let me help.... Sorry, my hands are like ice tonight. You know, it's funny—even when we were kids, nobody ever wanted me to touch them. It was like they thought they could catch a limp or something. I fell, trying to get on the bus the first day of school, and everybody laughed. Except Mother and Daddy, of course.

You were there, remember, in your nice pink dress and white patent leather shoes? I can still see you there. God, I always wanted shoes like that. I must have looked pretty funny, tumbling head over heels onto the street. I would have tried the bus again, just to be around other children—I even begged Mother to let me, but she and Daddy wouldn't hear of it. That's what

I really blame them for—loving me too much to let me live my own life. Love can be so destructive, can't it?

I spent every free moment with our piano—evenings, weekends, after school. I had lots of free time back then. I loved that piano. I guess it's why I love this picture. It's obvious how much she adores the piano—maybe as much as she loves him. Maybe more.

Stop giggling, I told you I hate that. It's true. You probably think I'm weird, but you could never understand the kind of loneliness I've lived with. It was awful, not having anyone my own age around. In fact, other than those times I spent in the hospital when they tried to fix my foot, and this summer here at the lake, I've never been away from my house for a whole night. You invited me to a slumber party once, when we were about ten, remember? Probably your parents made you ask me... yes, I thought so. Then the day of the party, my face swelled up from the mumps, and I couldn't go. I cried myself to sleep that night. And nobody ever invited me to a party again. Sometimes I was sure I'd die from the loneliness. I actually thought that might be possible. Now I know how silly that is; there are things much worse than loneliness.

But James changed all that this summer. He wasn't afraid to touch me. I was a little afraid at first and fought him off, but now I'm glad he insisted. The pain was worth it. But then, pain is always worth it. No, Daddy won't kill anybody when he finds out. He's used to his women betraying him. Anyway, he'll never find out now; it's too late. But I think in a way, it's always been too late.

No, that's not part of her dress, though it does look like it. No, it's part of the darkness hiding behind the draperies. Yes, there to the left. That's good. You seem to have a knack for puzzles, Heidi. Not everybody does, you know. It takes a special kind of talent, like music...or passion...or loneliness.

James knew about passion. He was the first person to ever show me any attention—except Mother and Daddy, of course. But that's all over now, since last night. Mother and Daddy had a birthday party for me out here—sweet seventeen. Only twenty-four hours ago, and it seems like a lifetime. Funny how time can do that, isn't it?

You sure you want to hear all this? All right, but don't say I didn't warn you—there's no turning back once I start the story. It's a very private story. Oh, I know you won't tell anyone.

No, no, that piece is part of her hand. Are you blind? His is rougher and stronger, a man's hand. Anyone can see the tendons and muscles stretched taut under his skin, as if he's getting ready for something important, something that will change him forever. Hers is delicate and limp, almost lifeless.

Anyway, as I was saying, everyone had left the lake house by ten last night after the party. It was a pretty dreary party, really, just friends of Mother's and Daddy's, since I didn't have any of my own to invite. And James—of course James was there. At least he stayed until all the others had gone home. Then he kissed me on the cheek—my parents were watching—wished me a happy birthday, and we said goodnight.

He went down the walkway to his bunk behind the boathouse. I lay awake for more than an hour, to make sure Mother and Daddy were really asleep. Then I tiptoed downstairs in my bare feet. I went out the back door and along the wooden sidewalk toward the garage. The boards were damp and slimy, and I nearly slipped a couple of times, because my balance is very bad, especially without my shoes. But I didn't care. I was going to see James, and I didn't want to take a chance on waking my parents with those big, clumping shoes.

Wait, give me that piece. It's where their lips are pressed together. I'll put it in. I don't like anybody else to touch that one.

Anyway, I opened the back door to the garage and went into James's room. I sat down on the mattress, near his head. He was snoring, but I thought he was only pretending to be asleep, because he'd been waiting for me. I just sat there for a long time, looking around and inhaling the scent of his cologne. I'd never been in his room before; usually he came to me.

When I reached out to stroke his hair, I noticed a photograph on his night table. It was a girl's picture. I must have gasped or jumped off the bed or something. I don't really remember.

Anyway, James opened his eyes and squinted at me. "What are you doing in here?" he asked.

His voice was scratchy and rough, kind of sexy. He'd really been asleep, not faking it, and somehow that made me angry. It wasn't part of my fantasy.

"I wanted to be with you," I answered. "I thought you cared about me."

But by then, I knew he didn't, not really. I just couldn't think of what else to say. I was shaking all over...yeah, kind of like I am right now. I picked up the photograph and threw it against the wall. The sound was almost deafening; glass seemed to explode everywhere, even inside my head.

He sat up and told me to get out; his voice wasn't sexy anymore. I'd never seen him that way before; it was kind of scary, the way his eyes narrowed and his fists clenched. I thought I'd caught him off guard, half-asleep like that. I told him I loved him, that I'd make him love me more than the girl in the photograph, if he'd just give me the chance. He told me I was crazy and called me nasty names. Then I think I begged him. I know I threatened him. I said I'd make sure my father ruined him forever if he didn't love me.

No, no, that piece won't fit there; don't try to force it. You'll ruin it if you try to force it. It's just background, anyway.

You know who was in the photograph, don't you? Don't try to act innocent now; it's too late. You probably gave him the picture after one of your dates. Did he tell you about our little kisses? Did you both have a good laugh about the silly, desperate crippled girl? Never mind, it doesn't matter.

What matters is what James did during our fight. He didn't tell you this yet, did he? He hasn't had the chance. Maybe that's why he called for you to meet him here.... Yes, I was listening, I know about that. I know about a lot of things, for a girl who doesn't get out much.

There, that's the last piece. It's all together, passionate and painful and beautiful and whole, like the end of a fairy tale. Now I'll tell you the end of my story, but it doesn't have anything to do with "happily ever after."

James threw me down on the floor and clutched my hair. He kept cursing me and hitting my head against the boards. I could feel tiny pieces of glass embedding themselves in my scalp, but he was so strong I couldn't stop him. I couldn't even yell. I must have blacked out. The next thing I knew, I was underwater, struggling to breathe, to find my way to the air. The water was pitch black, but the moon lit the surface. The way it does tonight. Only it looks much prettier from up here.

Of course I didn't know how to swim, and James knew that. James knew almost everything about me from our long talks when Mother and Daddy were gone. He was in the canoe above me. He had no trouble grabbing me from the side of the canoe every time I reached the surface, and pushing me under again and again every time I struggled to the air.

Finally, I realized struggling would only tire me out; I was going to drown. So I drew in a huge lungful of water, and sank down to the murky bottom. Drowning isn't so bad, really, once you surrender to it. It's like wrapping yourself in a wet blanket forever. You even get used to the cold after a while. And there are lots of others down there, too, to keep you company.

I felt something else, other than the dirt and water filling my lungs, as I sank deeper and deeper and my body instinctively twitched, fighting death for those last few seconds. I sensed movement all around me, a heavy shifting. I thought it came from some large fish, heading in for a meal when I finally gave up. But it was more than that—and less than that. The water and silt and stones themselves seemed to be quaking, groping toward me. I had never been so afraid, and at the same time, so eager.

In a moment, it was over. At that second, when life drifts away like the last bubble of breath, they entered me. I don't know who they are or why they want me, but I'm theirs now. I hold their fury and venom—and passion. Yes, there's passion there, too. I feel like someone else, like a hundred someone elses.

And death does have certain advantages. It took almost twenty-four hours, but I made it back. I don't even limp anymore, see? My clothes and hair have dried. James was surprised by my strength, too, when I dragged him down to the water after he finished his phone call to you. I didn't want to interrupt a lovers' chat. After all, as Mother always says, it's better to kill two birds with one stone....

James made a terrible commotion, but he's quiet now, and he understands me much better. You might as well stop screaming, Heidi, we're all alone out here. Come on, we have to go down to the lake now; you don't want to keep James and the others waiting.

Lisa Lepovetsky is widely published in the genres of mystery and dark fiction and poetry. She has work in more than 200 publications, including Cemetery Dance magazine, Ellery Queen's Mystery Magazine, Disturbed Digest and many others, as well as dozens of anthologies: Dark Destiny, Crossroads in the Dark, Blood Muse, etc. She earned her MFA from Penn State and has taught for them and the U. of Pittsburgh. She lives in the mountains of PA.

CROSS-CONTAMINATION

HOLLY SCHOFIELD

I let my sister step into the dome airlock ahead of me. Our sons had cycled through already. In the tiny lock, with Liz's faceplate only centimeters from mine, I hit the red button to start the cycle. Her mouth tightened when I dampened the old pink towel with bleach and kicked it against the bottom edge of the deteriorating outer door.

"It keeps enough of the spores out." I shrugged, my enviro-suit creaking in response. "And I *will* fix it when the next harvest is sold."

She frowned and crossed her arms. "Caro, you—"

I held up a finger. With an audible whoosh, Devonia's lethal CO_2-rich outer atmosphere was sucked out and, in the partial vacuum that remained, decontamination spray—a mixture of my own design—shot out of the jets. It surrounded our puffed-out suits like a tropical storm, cleansing off spores and bacteria from the planet's surface and from Liz's skimmer interior.

After a minute, the lock refilled itself with air from the oxygen production plant attached to my domes.

When the light turned green and the inner door swung open, Liz entered the loading bay and began to remove her slick new enviro-suit. I picked up the spray bottle that stood on the metal bench, glad to see drops still spotted the floor from when Parag and Saje had passed through minutes ago. Good lad. Despite Parag's excitement at Saje's visit, he'd still taken time for proper decontam.

Liz stepped out of her suit and hung it on a hook. "Caro, you can't live like—"

I sprayed her in the chest.

"What the hell!"

"New procedure. Turn around, lift your arms. Who knows what germs you brought from P-town? You're lucky I don't make you strip."

She sputtered but complied, managing to incorporate sarcasm into her arm motions. "You know I try not to give you advice, Caro."

"And I appreciate it." I handed her the spray bottle and gestured she should spray me.

"But sometimes...well, you have to realize that you come across as a bit..."

"Weird? Obsessive? Deranged?"

"Different. Let's go with 'different'." She spritzed my knees a bit more aggressively than needed.

"A husband dead from community negligence will do that to a person." I did a little shimmy so the spray would dry off more quickly and strode past her.

She followed me into the kitchen, running her fingers through her fashionable buzz cut, flicking away drops of decontamination spray. "It's been ten years, sis."

I settled at the table and began sorting through the bins of freshly picked basil. She didn't get it. She didn't get that civilization had let me down; that here, four hours by skimmer from P-town, in the middle of Devonia's desert-like landscape, there might be danger but it was predictable, manageable danger. More so than P-town's, anyway.

"Crime rate's up, I hear," I said, sorting the not-quite-perfect basil leaves from the glossier ones I could sell to upscale P-town restaurants.

"Not much on a per capita basis. The population's up, too, you know. There're more job opportunities. You might be able to get your old job back."

I didn't even dignify that with an answer. Like I'd want to go back to bylaw enforcement when I was perfectly happy—perfectly *safe*—here, growing my own food, raising Parag to be a self-sufficient, careful person.

"Caro, let me lend you a few credits. You can fix the airlock, update your enviro-suits, and pay me back whenever."

"No!" Damn it, I felt a hot flash starting, triggered by stress: a common side-effect seeing Liz. I usually kept her visits and our vid conversations short. Why had I ever invited my nephew, Saje, to stay for the weekend? Sure enough, a wall of heat washed over me. I closed my eyes for a moment, letting Chi-Gong breathing techniques take over. Sometimes they helped; this time, dizziness started in my temples and rushed downward. I could practically feel my surface blood vessels dilating. Menopause is not for sissies.

Liz was still talking, watching my flushed face. "You don't need to suffer like that. I can supply you with RightTher pills, anytime you want. Proven technology." Two years farther into perimenopause than me, she'd offered me hormone therapy drugs several times before.

I gave my usual answer through gritted teeth. "So they say, despite a bit of contrary evidence and some inconclusive studies. Those drugs tamper with more than estrogen levels, Liz. Until they're better understood, I'll stay organic."

She snorted. "Two hundred years of hormone therapy studies aren't enough for you, huh? And neither are super-thick floor braces in all sectors of P-town." She had the grace to look abashed at that and added, "Sorry."

I watched my knuckles turn white on the table edge. I'd been widowed when Parag was three. Rajit had been killed along with ten others when an upper story of P-town's central dome had given away due to shoddy construction materials.

"I intend on living out here for Parag's sake as well as my own," I ground out. Even if Devonia's frontier laws recognized a thirteen-year-old as an adult, I didn't. I'd keep him here through high school—three more years. After that, it was beyond my control. The thought of him leaving our homestead as an adult made me break out in sweat all over again.

"Did you ask her? Did you?" Parag's large feet almost caught the edge of a chair as he barged into the kitchen. He brushed tousled black hair out of his eyes, banging an elbow on the wall in the process.

Despite my irritation with Liz, I couldn't help smiling at him and his gawkiness. Thirteen is such a tough age.

But then, so is fifty. I wiped beaded sweat off my forehead. The hot flash was finishing; I'd have to remember to add this episode—along with three during the night—to the chart I was keeping.

"Time I gave you a haircut," I said. "Did I ask Liz what?"

But he was looking at Liz, not me. "Not yet," she answered. "I haven't had a—"

"Ask me what?" I interrupted. What the *hell!* Liz has been talking to Parag behind my back?

"Ask'er yourself, toenail." Saje, my nephew, sauntered into the kitchen accompanied by his usual scowl, his metallic scalp tats, and silly cheek jewels. He elbowed Parag, hard enough to make him grimace. At thirteen-and-a-half, lanky Saje oozed coolness—*zeit*, the kids called it now. Parag idolized him. I didn't trust him a micron. After Liz had talked me into letting him visit, I'd spoken to Parag for a couple of hours, trying to inoculate him against peer pressure, trust in authority, complacency with his surroundings—all the things that lead to danger.

Parag's tawny cheeks turned the color of a ripe Sunny Brown tomato. "High school, Mom. Can I stay with Aunt Liz and Saje and attend school

IRL? Can I? I'll work hard, Aunt Liz says it's okay with her. I'll be perfectly safe. I'll watch out for all of P-town's dangers. Can I?" His voice rose as his statements became more and more absurd.

"Out of the question, Parag." I put down the clump of basil I was holding, gently, softly, in perfect control. "If people could keep themselves safe in P-town just by being wary, your father would still be alive."

My statement, logical as it was, made all of them cringe. I couldn't help that. Rajit and I had immigrated here as newlyweds, choosing Devonia over the other colonized planets, willing to adjust to the slightly higher gravity. Of the available choices, it was the most geologically calm planet with the least nasty flora and fauna. We'd done everything we could to have the safest environment possible. I banished the image of Rajit's bruised and bleeding face surrounded by flashing medi-unit equipment.

"Mom, please..." Parag grabbed my sleeve.

I froze, keeping my face in control.

His jaw tightened and he scowled just like Saje. "I'm going. Next month. And you can't stop me."

"We'll see about that." I gave him what I privately called "the evil eye" and calmly plucked off a yellowed basil leaf, adding it to the small pile of detritus.

Saje sucked on his teeth. "Leave it 'lone for now, toenail. She'll come 'round. C'mon, let's go play vids and 'gram up some food. 'M starving." He pulled Parag back toward the main dome. I didn't say a word, even a moment later when Saje turned the vid volume up loud enough to vibrate the walls.

Liz clucked her tongue. "Parag just wants a bit of freedom, Caro. Cooped up in here..." She trailed off at my look.

"Liz, the next three years with my son are as precious as the first three. I need him here. And he needs to be here." A third hot flash rose from my chest, this time like instant heartburn. I leaned back, mustering the energy to speak. "Go, Liz. Go harass somebody else. See you tomorrow." I flapped a hand limply and closed my eyes.

Without a word, Liz headed for the airlock, letting the hiss of the door speak for her.

I decided to leave the boys' safety protocol lesson until later. Parag was too upset to listen and, due to the draining after-effects of the hot flashes, I didn't have the energy it would take to get Saje's attention. Besides, I needed to identify some greenish spores I'd swabbed off the edge of Liz's skimmer door.

Evolving in a similar mild fashion to Earth's Devonian epoch, this planet—the well-named Devonia—held only predictable, stable risks. Vascular plants had not yet evolved flowers, or even roots or leaves. They replicated via sporangia, sending clouds of colorful spores across the rifts and valleys that lay just outside my trio of domes. Stringy stems of harmless mosses formed prairies that stretched for thousands of kilometers.

Bacteria, lichens, and green algae made up the rest of the ecosystem, along with wingless insects and worms, all busy creating the cryptobiotic soil that would drastically transform this world in a hundred million years or so. No mammals, no vermin, no predators. Except humans, all two hundred thousand of us: colonists, entrepreneurs, farmers, and incompetent building contractors.

The biggest threats to me and Parag out here on Marmalade Ridge were various molds and mildews attacking the greenhouse crops. Using UV lights that I'd modified for disinfection had been, so far, effective.

The analyzer beeped and I scrolled through the report. A few spikes in the quantities of fungal spores but nothing I hadn't already gotten under control in the greenhouse.

I suppressed a sudden shiver. Coming off a hot flash was like recovering from the flu—my internal thermostat wouldn't read right for a bit. I didn't turn up the 20C dome temperature; I was determined not to let this phase of life affect my daily tasks.

Especially the safety protocol lecture. I pushed back my chair. If Parag and Saje weren't ready to listen, I'd just have to make them.

They were still sprawled in front of the vid screen. Judging from their empty plates and bowls, they'd shoved in an enormous amount of food. Saje must like my homegrown organic veggies. He lay slumped sideways on the sofa, looking even more bored than usual. I was sure Parag had talked him into this visit, and Liz had probably felt that Parag needed companionship. Which I had no doubt he did, but Saje was far from my ideal choice. I decided to ignore Parag's ultimatum—after Saje left, I'd make him come around to my way of thinking.

"Come on, boys." I paid no attention to their groans and started my lecture, simplifying Parag's weekly ones down to essentials. A tour of the greenhouse's weak spots made them perk up and they came up with several disaster scenarios I hadn't really considered, most of them bloody and explosive. We ended up at the airlock. I started a lecture on the enviro-suits' limitations but Parag rolled his eyes before I even got the rack components listed.

"Three suits, Mom. We can count." He gestured at our two worn-out suits and Saje's trendy tighter one. "Are we done yet? We got better stuff to do."

"Yeah, there mus' be *something* fun to do 'round here," Saje looked around in an exaggerated way. He tapped the corridor viewscreen, changing it from translucent to transparent, over and over.

I forbade myself to slap his hand. "Look, do a check on all three suits and then I'll cut you loose until dinner." I'd bought both our rebuilt suits from the same old miner that had sold me the domes ten years ago. He'd bought them used from a spacer so constant inspections were necessary, until I had the cash from next month's tomato crops. We both needed new clothes too. Parag's shirts had four extensions in the sleeves, odd colored rings at his wrist where my aging 3D printer couldn't quite match the original fabric color. The printer had come with the domes too. I'd left everything behind after Rajit's death, quitting my job, cashing in my savings for these three rehabbed domes and the 100-year leasehold on Marmalade Ridge.

"Hey, Caro, can we go outside?" Saje lost some of his oh-so-cool P-town zeit as he looked through the viewscreen, twisting a cheek jewel around and around. Beyond the skimmer landing pad, fields of marmalade-toned fungi spread for kilometers, studded with various taller plants, blending to a gray-green blur in the distance.

Parag shoved up next to him. "See those shiny cup-shaped fungi?" He pointed a few meters away. "*Coronaria*, the scientists call 'em. They pick up minerals from the soil as protection so that they're inedible to worms and stuff. Right, mom?"

"D'ya have to confirm *everything* with her, toenail?" Saje blew out his lips. "And get permission t' do everything?"

Parag flushed and jabbed a thumb at the screen, switching the view to the far side of the main dome. The old miner had built these domes on a cliff edge, safety be damned, letting the mine tailings fall downslope—out of sight and mind, I suppose. On the far horizon, snow-capped mountains gleamed. "Can we go out, Mom? I can show Saje the view of the Valley. Please, Mom? Just Saje and me?"

An unnecessary risk. I didn't take those. I started to shake my head, then reconsidered. Maybe I should let them go out. Parag would see Saje's lack of bush-smarts and poor impulse control. Saje would get in some mild sort of trouble and Parag would rescue him. If it helped Parag to see Saje for what he was, it might make him decide against high school in P-town. In the long run, it might actually save his life. I twisted my wedding ring around and around my finger before, Gaia help me, I nodded.

Parag whooped with delight.

I gripped my nephew's shoulders. "Saje, I need you to look right at me and tell me that you understand this is not P-town and we are four hours from a hospital. The outside can kill you as soon as look at you. No games. Do you read?" Parag had done several solo hikes and there wasn't much that could go wrong but a little exaggeration couldn't hurt.

"Yeah, Caro. I'm zeit." Saje's eyes held sincerity. I hoped.

"Well, if you do the three suit checks and you stay well back from the cliff edge and you do half-hour radio check-ins and, Parag, you tell Saje all about cross-contamination and—"

"—decontam procedures when we come back in. Yeah, I know, Mom. Quit taking all the fun out of it." That scowl again.

I gave them both an equally stern look and headed off to my greenhouse workbench.

It was going to be a long couple of days.

The pipette I held dripped on the countertop and I realized I'd been staring into space for several minutes. I placed it back in its stand and turned off the analyzer, no farther ahead in my task of hybridizing a Peach Fuzz tomato with a Sunny Brown to make it more marketable to upper-income P-town taste buds. My savings and Rajit's life insurance payout were almost exhausted and I was hoping to expand my basil sales to include tomatoes, using Liz as the courier.

I glanced at my wrist display, surprised to see twenty minutes had gone by. My time sense was off, another classic symptom of menopause. Nine minutes until the boys' first check-in. I'd restricted them to a radius of one kilometer, figuring that would be safe enough. Parag would radio in at the exact minute—he was responsible and strong, the way he needed to be.

I jumped when Parag's familiar double-bell rang out three minutes early. Early meant trouble. I stood up, tapping my console to accept the transmission, even as a head rush rose unbidden. What had I been thinking, letting them go outside alone?

"Mom? Mom! Do you read? Over." The radio crackled but the excitement in his voice was clear.

"Any injuries?"

"I can't—" Saje's voice dissolved into crackles.

I tweaked settings but the static remained.

"I'll be right there. Out." Damn! Something was wrong. I hurried, cramming back into my suit, stepping into the airlock as I sealed my helmet, glad the boys had done decontamination procedures as part of their suit checks. I didn't have the ten minutes it would take to spray decontam gas on the way out.

I booted the pink towel aside as the airlock opened outwards, remembering to grab an emerg backpack at the last second. A rush at my back as air pushed past me.

The pale orange carpet of fungus crunched beneath my boots as I broke into a trot. A purple slime mold decorated a boulder to my left and a tall blue-gray fungal tower loomed over me on my right, leaving a long shadow in the sunshine like some ancient Greek column.

"Report. Over." I said into my suit mike as soon as I'd cleared the lock. Saje must have taunted Parag, made him stick his arm in a hole in the rocks or something.

The radio was silent.

"Report, Parag, report!"

Nothing. Suit radios didn't have the strength of the dome's console; they had to be in line-of-sight. I looked around, rolling hills for at least a klick east past the skimmer pad and the same west in the direction of the very distant P-town. Nothing moved.

I ran past the skimmer pad, Devonia's 1.2 gees weighing down each step, trampling moss and other ground plants.

"Report! Parag! Over!"

Zzzzz. Saje's voice, fuzzy and faint.

And, almost overlapping: "*Zzzzz.* Coordinates West one five three seven, North niner six eight *zzzzz*—." Parag's voice. Thank Gaia!

I checked my wrist compass and skidded in my tracks, turning left, sending up little puffs of dirt. They were beside the domes, and an unknown distance north. Thank Gaia, too, that Parag had been listening when I'd taught him how to triangulate his coordinates, using his compass and a couple of the more distinctive mountain peaks.

I raced around the main dome network, skirting the greenhouse, plowing through the knee-high bed of moss that lay below the water vapor vents.

"*Zzzzz.* North niner six eight four. *Zzzzz.*" Parag again, still faint but clearer.

I stumbled over the candelabra shape of a menorah fungus, checking my compass again. In the 100-meter grid system we used, eight was quite a bit to the north. Saje must have convinced Parag to push the one-kilometer limit I'd set. I should never have let them go.

I was beginning to pant. Hustling over rough ground with a heavy pack was sucking away all the energy I had. I cranked up my oxygen although I'd determined a few months ago that O_2 was a hot flash trigger. Sure enough, in a few more steps, my ears rang and my head spun. My hypothalamus had cut loose, hot and heavy.

Never mind. I could do this. I trudged over hundreds of puffballs, the size of golf balls, sending up clouds of gray spores. Spores and bacteria were floating in the tropical heat all around me, invisibly invading any micron-sized breaches in my worn-out suit. I breathed shallowly for a bit then realized that was foolish—any spores would be in my lungs already.

Suddenly I was angry, really mad. Blast those boys! Parag would never leave the dome again, if I had anything to say about it. And I did.

I kicked some puffballs and made a conscious effort to relax. Maybe their injuries were minor. Maybe it would all be okay. At least, the boys had sterilized the outside of my suit: my microbiota wouldn't cross-contaminate the Devonia environment, although decontam was going to take forever when we got back.

Another few steps and I should be almost to the cliff edge, I thought, although several bushy menorah obscured my view. A glance at my compass and I grabbed a branch for support. A reading of North Nine Six Eight was far down the hill. They'd fallen off the cliff!

Uninvited, a memory filled my mind. Parag's toddler face, red and crying, one tiny arm wrapped around his father's leg as Rajit lay in the hospital bed that was his final resting place. I hadn't been able to save Parag from that but I could save him now.

"Almost there! Hold on!" I shouted, pushing through thick branches of menorah and twisting sideways between two unusually large tower fungi. My ancient suit rasped against their tough blue-gray hide. I forced myself to slow down. I didn't need a second disaster.

The cliff edge had to be close. Delicate fronds from a beige fernlike plant waved against my faceplate, obscuring my view.

"Oh, and when you get to the edge, watch out for the giant slime mold!" Parag's voice was strong and loud—a clear line-of-sight at last! His meaning registered just as my feet slid out from under me. A thump as my backside hit, a clunk as my shoulder knocked against a rock, then it was all a purple blur as I slid and slid and slid.

"Mom! Didn't you hear me warn you?" Parag's thin body rushed into view, then Saje's weedier figure walking more carefully behind. My feet were somehow pointing uphill and the emerg pack had slewed around to my side. I eased around until my feet were downslope and gingerly raised myself to a sitting position.

I had slid all the way down the huge expanse of slime mold, at least half a klick into the valley. The mold hadn't been there last week. How had it grown so large, so fast? I tried to grab a handful to collect a sample but my fingers stayed open.

"S'all zeit, Caro." Saje's voice was calm, almost laconic. "You could've stayed up top. We didn't need rescuing."

"Saje, shut up. She may be hurt. Mom, mom, are you okay?" Parag's voice squeaked like when he was nine years old and wracked with nightmares about his father's death.

"I'm okay, just let me sit a minute, honey. Hot flash." I shook my head, trying to clear the heavy drumbeat from my ears. I cranked up my suit fan and lowered my thermostat watching the digits on my wrist display flick by: twenty-two degrees C, twenty, eighteen.

While Parag explained to Saje why a woman in this day and age would choose to experience the full effects of menopause, I tried to gather up the energy to stand. I waited for the wash of sweet relief from the temperature change. It didn't come. Hot flashes sometimes lasted ten minutes. How long had I been sitting here?

I craned up at the long, long slope and the curve of the main dome far above. "How did you ever climb down here in just twenty minutes?"

"We came down on those Coro-whatevers. So zeit! I can't believe how fun it was!" Saje said. A corner of my mind noted that his voice held excitement for the first time today. He gestured at the heftiest *Coronaria* I had ever seen, a silvery saucer-shaped disc at least a meter in diameter.

"You rode down on fungus? Have you lost your minds?" Turning to face Parag made my vision swim. "Saje suggested it and you went along, right? Son, you—"

Parag's helmet jerked upright. "No, Mom. It was my idea. I wanted to try sliding down the hill, like they do on snow sleds in the vids. I didn't know they'd be so zeit and travel so far."

"S'true." Saje cut in, his cheek jewel glinting through his faceplate. "I told'm not to. Then I followed'm 'cause I didn't want'm down here 'lone."

"Sorry, Mom. Nobody's hurt. Can we head back now? I want to upload some pics."

I was so hot, I just nodded and got slowly to my feet. Saje slung the emerg pack on his shoulder and they both raced off, grabbing at boulders, pulling themselves up the cliff through the gravel and glistening muck. My helmet rang with excited shouts about slime and metals and experiments they could do when they got back. I took one step. I was drenched in sweat although my internal suit temp said 15C. I turned my suit conditioner down another five degrees.

Another step and the world tilted. "Boys, wait!" The shout took everything I had and left me nauseated. I sat down heavily on a small rock, mashing the fawn-colored lichens that clung to the top.

"You don't have to shout, Mom. It's a radio. Are you okay?" Parag's voice was loud in my helmet even though they had both already climbed about thirty meters upslope.

My vision swayed like that time I'd tried freefall. I checked the thermostat again then thought to check the actual internal thermometer. 40C. Somehow, the thermostat was overriding my cooler setting. "My suit, it's overheating."

I closed my eyes as I listened to the two boys slithering back down the slope.

"We need to cool her down. Look at her face, it's as red as a beefsteak tomato!" Parag's high-pitched voice seemed very far away.

"Any ideas?" Saje's voice. I was glad the question wasn't directed at me. I was about to fall off the rock.

"Saje, we blew it. We didn't do the suit check," Parag whispered.

"Shut up, toenail," Saje whispered back.

Whispering into the radio so I wouldn't overhear—I knew that ought to be funny, but I couldn't exactly get my mind around why.

"I thought Mom would double-check the suits. She always does." Parag sounded near tears.

I had just enough mental marbles to grok the irony in that. My own careful vigilance of Parag had led to less quality control than no supervision at all.

Saje's voice got louder. "We need t' cool her down. C'n we get ice from somewhere?" He was probably looking up at the white-topped mountains hundreds of miles away. The thought of snow was heavenly.

Parag's feet crunched on loose gravel. "There're cenotes farther down the slope, maybe two klicks. Can we get her there and maybe submerge her?"

I pictured them dragging me two thousand meters. My antique suit would wear through before we were out of sight of the slime mold. The question was, why was my suit overheating? I tried to picture the suit's HVAC system. My mental wiring diagram seemed to have a mind of its own: coils of wires writhing and twisting like snakes, capacitors grinning evilly. Like my own menopausally malfunctioning thermostat, chips overheating, smugly and without remorse.

I brought a hand up to wipe my very wet face and it clunked against my helmet. I was getting delirious. I bit my lip until I tasted blood, hoping the pain would make me focus.

I leaned back on the rock. What if the suit wasn't overheating, but simply reacting to its environment? Triggered like my hot flashes? Loss of control. Maybe it was all about loss of control.

"Mom, Mom, do you read? Over, over, damn..."

How long had Parag been calling me?

"More heat," I said. "Make me hotter. Light a fire, maybe."

"Mom? That doesn't make any sense. Can you stand and walk?"

"Caro?" Saje's voice. "Parag, she looks worse."

I mumbled my explanation. "These suits are built for emergency deep space work—they heat up if they sense the exterior is bitterly cold. I think my *external* sensor is wonky. If it gets hot enough, the *internal* sensor may allow itself to lower in compensation."

"Zeit..." Parag breathed as Saje exclaimed, "Foolin' the suit! That's brill!"

"If we can create a spark, make a fire near the sensor..." I trailed off, hoping they could figure out what I meant. A campfire, burning fungus like it was peat, might do the trick.

"A fire? Mom, you're not thinking straight. A fire in Dev's atmosphere?"

He was right. There wasn't enough oxygen to start a fire, much less keep one going.

"Mom!" Parag was shaking me, almost sobbing. "Mom, listen. I've got an idea. The *Coronaria* look like parabola. They'll have a focal point, maybe. They can concentrate the sunlight!"

Through my fogged faceplate, the nearest huge fungus beckoned, curved like an old-fashioned beanbag chair. Like a satellite dish. It *could* work.

I nodded and my head swam. "Help me over to it, help me." My weak voice must have held some remnant of parental command: hands pulled me forward. I slumped to my knees and put a hand out where the shiny surface reflected a bright patch of sunlight. I held my wrist about half of a meter above it and used the suit's light meter to measure the luminescence at what I guessed was the focal spot. The numbers flickered. 50,000 lux. Not enough. "Move my wrist until it reads the highest."

Parag shifted my arm and after a few tries, he squeaked, "75,000 lux, Mom."

"Good," I breathed out. Formulae slipped and slid through my head but I thought that should translate to a fairly high temperature.

Where was the external sensor? My upper arm? "Lift me up so I can lean across the dish." The world spun as they draped me awkwardly over it. I angled my bicep into the focal spot.

A couple of minutes went by. I think I might have moaned.

"It's not working, Saje. She's gonna die." Parag's terror was palpable. He wasn't as strong as I thought.

"Shut up and hand me some of that rubbery-looking fungus, the black gunk o'er there."

"What? Why?"

"To make the sensor darker. Darker absorbs heat better. Give it over and I'll smear some on."

Hands grasped my arm and twisted it uncomfortably then repositioned it.

A curious peace settled over me. Whatever happened next, it was out of my control. Oddly, I felt freer now than I had since Rajit had died. Something released deep inside me, cleansing, purifying. The situation would end, somehow. I'd survive.

Or I wouldn't.

Time hovered.

Suddenly, sweet relief as my suit's air conditioner kicked on, full blast. I held back tears as my sweat dried and my faceplate cleared. Within minutes, I was happily shaking with cold.

When Liz barged in, I was sitting at the kitchen table, sipping an iced tea made with hips from my *Rosa villosa* roses and pure H_2O.

"Are you *sure* Saje is okay? And Parag? Tell me to my face."

I'd messaged her just as she'd walked in the door of her P-town apartment, then I'd relayed our little adventure to her as she drove the skimmer here in record time.

"It's all under control now," I said for the tenth time and took another sip. I held the glassful—my sixth since we'd returned—against my temple. I still couldn't seem to get cool enough even though the medi-unit said I was fine. It also said my endorphins were higher than my ten-year norm.

I smiled at my sister, at the worried frown that spoiled the lines in her well-preserved face. She had my well-being, and the kids, at heart. Out there at the bottom of the slope, my perceptions of her had reset, along with my suit controls.

I took another sip. Maybe it was time I reset my perceptions about Saje, too.

The boys burst into the kitchen, all shouts and hugs, and began their own rambling explanation of events. I let them blather on, downplaying my suit malfunction and up-playing their own part in the rescue.

"All right, that's enough," I finally said. "I did think I was going to go to sleep out there. Permanently. But now, now I've woken up."

Across from me, Liz sucked in her breath.

Parag held himself very still, cheeks tinged with red.

"No, Parag. I'm not ready to let you go to P-town for high school. I'm simply not." I held up a hand forestalling his next words. "However." I cleared my throat and turned to Saje. "However, I would like you to stay longer, Saje, if you want to. For the week?"

"Uh, I got tix for that Sly Shoomba concert, and Melanie was goin' to take me to..." He trailed off as Liz gave him her own version of the evil eye.

I chose my words carefully. "Saje, you showed real self-control out there. And Parag showed some quick thinking. I think you and Parag can learn from each other."

Saje shrugged. "Zeit, okay, for a few days." He nudged Parag. "Let out your breath now, toenail."

With a happy whoop, Parag hugged me and ran off to his room. Saje winked at me before sauntering after him.

Liz tilted her head. "It's a start."

"You know," I said, mopping my face with a hand towel, "Back when I was in bylaw enforcement, we were taught that we couldn't regulate everything all the time. It seems I'd forgotten that."

She waved a hand. "Must be menopause brain, makes you forget everything."

She caught my thrown hand towel before it hit her chest, her teeth glinting like Saje's cheek jewels. "Careful, Caro, you're spreading germs."

I grinned at her and reached over to 'gram her an iced tea. "He's a good kid, Saje is. You raised him well. And P-town isn't all bad." I caught her eye. "That doesn't mean I've decided about Parag and high school. I'm still thinking on it."

She took the glass from me. "Fine, let's leave it at that. I still have some questions, though. The *Coronaria* grew so large here because why?" Liz raised an eyebrow.

I swallowed some tea. "I figure it's because they digested the mine tailings piled outside. The unnatural concentration of minerals stimulated their growth and gave them an extra reflective surface. But I have to say I don't understand why the slime mold is so extensive. It's a bit worrying."

"I can answer that," Liz said, "It's the effect of P-town. It's happening in all the valleys around here, wherever we have effluent leaking out from the domes. The recyclers are very very good but they're certainly not perfect. And they're getting strained now as the population grows. You'd know that if you kept up with the news."

I snorted and drew a circle on the table using the moisture from my glass. From the size of the tower fungi near the dome, I'd already figured there must be a tiny leak in my own effluent system too. "What did you expect? There's no such thing as perfect control."

When the airlock door hissed shut behind Liz, Saje immediately flooded the dome speakers with some awful jangling music. I supposed I'd grow used to the noise, but for now, it was a bit stressful. Sure enough, a flash of heat washed over me. I smiled ruefully and 'grammed another iced tea, prepared to ride it out.

Holly Schofield travels through time at the rate of one second per second, oscillating between the alternate realities of city and country life. Her fiction has been published in Lightspeed's "Women Destroy Science Fiction", AE, Unlikely Stories, Tesseracts, and many other venues throughout the world. For more of her work, see hollyschofield.wordpress.com/.

UNRAVELING

K.G. ANDERSON

"Sarah—he's using you!" My voice rose into the whine my daughter loathed, but I couldn't stop. I pressed the phone to my ear. "You're 16. I absolutely forbid —"

My runaway daughter informed me that she hated me.

"Have fun with the old witches," she said, and hung up.

I climbed out of the car, slammed the battered door, and slumped against the sun-baked metal. Gradually my heartbeat slowed, but still felt frighteningly uneven. Fail-ure, fail-ure, FAIL-ure, it thumped.

A crow cawed and a soft breeze rustled the pine trees surrounding my great-aunts' summer cottage. I thought about phoning Sarah's father for help, but my ex had long since given up on our daughter.

I reached through the open car window, pulled out my shabby purse and rummaged savagely for my cigarettes until I remembered I'd quit smoking two months ago. The sounds of kids playing drifted up from the lake.

"All-y all-y in come free," sang a little girl. Squeals of excitement. Someone shrieked, "Mom-my!"

Sarah? Of course not. My Sarah hadn't played here in years. A hot tear splashed on my blouse, soaking through to my breast. I wiped my cheeks and glanced over at the old cottage. Two metal chairs stood empty on the sagging front porch.

My great-aunts Helen and Nessie were inside, playing Rummy and waiting for me. I'd gone into town to get us food for dinner: A rotisserie chicken and a package of rolls. Nessie would overcook some vegetables "to go with."

I pulled the bag of groceries from the back seat and crossed the pine needle lawn, pasting a smile on my face that claimed everything's fine. I mentally rehearsed telling them that Sarah was working an internship at an art gallery in the city, that she'd wished she could come visit. If only.

Their hearts would have broken to hear her call them old witches.

The screen door slammed behind me and Helen and Nessie looked up from the Rummy melds they had spread on the kitchen table.

"Finish, finish," I said.

By the time I'd put the groceries away, Helen was picking up the cards. Nessie made a pot of tea. She poured me a cup, slopping a bit onto the saucer.

"Ellie! What's wrong?" She drew a finger along her cheek, mirroring the tear track she'd noticed on mine.

I shrugged. "Oh, it's Sarah. You know. Teenagers." I couldn't bear to tell them the truth.

"I picked up your mail," I said, eager to change the subject. Reaching into my purse I pulled out a batch of envelopes and put them on the table. "Did you go down to the beach while I was in town?"

"The beach?" Helen's laugh ended in a sigh. "The beach? Oh, Ellie, we're a little old for that."

"I don't think we've gone to the beach since Reba died," Nessie said. "We sit out on the porch in the mornings."

Reba, the youngest of the great aunts, had died two years ago, and since, her sisters had aged rapidly. Their lakeside house, for so many years the gathering place for the Steins and Kettermens, had grown shabby and quiet. Everyone seemed to be too busy to visit them.

"That bastard."

Nessie, her lips pursed, thrust a letter at Helen. "Look at this. The momzer."

Helen took the page, adjusted her glasses, and read quickly. Then she tossed the letter onto the table.

"So, Ellie, your cousin Harold's making us sell the house," she said. "Living up here at the lake is 'too much' for us, he says. He thinks we'd like a nursing home better."

Nellie growled, "Reba must be spinning in her grave!"

"Oh." I felt guilty. I already knew about Harold's plan. He'd called me and tried to enlist me in his scheme to get at their property. I wondered if the great-aunts knew how valuable their land had become, with million-dollar weekend retreats going up all around them. If they let Harold handle the deal, they'd never find out. I'd never liked Harold much, but I wasn't about to get in the middle of this family drama.

"It's hard to imagine you moving out of this house," I said.

The great-aunts exchanged looks.

"That's what we want to talk to you about," said Nessie.

"Moving?" I was confused. "I wish the house could stay in the family, but I couldn't possibly buy it. After my divorce..."

Nessie flapped a large, be-ringed hand at me.

"No, no," she said. "No, it's...Helen, we need to show her."

"After dinner," Helen said.

The cold roasted chicken was accompanied by Nellie's thoroughly boiled green beans and followed by coffee ice cream, our family favorite.

I cleared the table and, over their protests, washed the plates and put them in the counter-top dish strainer, just as I'd done hundreds of times before. Then I made a fresh pot of tea. But when I brought it to the table, Nessie stood up and gestured to me. I followed the two old girls as they shuffled down the hallway toward the living room.

I was trying to imagine what they had to show me. A quilt, maybe? A lamp? Some old family heirloom that had miraculously survived all the summers with the cousins up here?

But Nessie surprised me by stopping halfway down the hall. She fished a key from her apron pocket. Fumbling, she unlocked a door in the hallway. A closet I'd never noticed? She opened the door to reveal a narrow staircase of worn painted wood. She leaned out over the stairs to pull a string and a bare light bulb, the fixture high on the wall, came on.

"I'm going to let her look," Nessie said to Helen.

Look at what? I wondered.

"Go on."

They stood back and I went down the dim stairs, grasping the thin metal railing attached to the wall on the left side. To my right was open space and darkness. Apparently this cellar had no windows. That would explain why the cousins and I had never seen it from outside the house.

I peered into the depths, my eyes gradually adjusting to the dimness. The staircase went down not to a floor but into a sea of what appeared to be tangled foliage. I hesitated, went down two more steps, and bent down to touch the odd material. It seemed to be string, or rope, or some sort of dark yarn. There appeared to be bushels of it. There was no telling how deep it went; the staircase vanished into it like a spoon in a pot of soup. A smell of old, slightly damp wool drifted up from the tangles. I sniffed cautiously and wrinkled my nose.

I turned and looked back up at Nessie, silhouetted by the red evening light at the top of the stairs.

"What on earth is this stuff?" I asked.

"Come back up and we'll explain," said Nessie. She sounded tired.

I hurried up, relieved when Nessie locked that door behind us. We returned to the kitchen table.

Nessie seemed reluctant to start. She gestured toward the teapot and I poured for her and for me, Helen having shaken her head and taken up her knitting.

"Ellie, do you remember Cousin Esther?" Nessie asked as I drank from my cup.

"*Shweig*," Helen interrupted. She stood up and lumbered in her black orthopedic sandals to the back door and closed it. "Someone might hear!"

When Helen returned to the table, Nessie began again. "Cousin Esther was a woman disappointed with her life."

I brushed some crumbs away from my elbows and leaned forward, puzzled. I had a vague memory of Esther, elegant and sour. But what could she have to do with the vast sea of yarn in the cellar?

"It started out so well for Esther," Nessie said. "A good marriage to a lovely man, a Yiddisher kopf with a good business. Esther had three children, but her favorite was her daughter, Shulamit."

Nessie stared at me. "Don't you remember, Ellie? Don't you remember about Shulamit?"

Suddenly it all came back to me. I was a kid when it happened, but I remembered my mother going pale when she read the paper at the breakfast table. It was just a few months after Shulamit had married the senator's son. They were flying in his private plane to Martha's Vineyard. The plane went down in Long Island Sound. There were no survivors.

"The plane crashed," I said softly as Nessie and Helen nodded. "Shulamit died. Cousin Esther, she went crazy with grief."

"That's not exactly what happened to Esther."

Across the table, Helen stopped knitting and cast a worried look at the door.

Nessie leaned close.

"Esther went to the Treyad," she said, "and asked for another life."

"The Treyad? The witches? Poor woman," I said. "She'd really gone nuts."

"Not so much," said Nessie. "Ellie, in those days those witches were powerful. People came to them for a new life, and—poof!" Nessie rocked her squat body back in her chair. "They vanished."

I'd had about enough of this witches nonsense. The great-aunts had been born in the old country; they still believed in the Treyad. As kids we'd been frightened of the stories—about three women with the power to unravel your life and make you start over again.

Oh, if only!

"You know, I don't remember Cousin Esther vanishing," I told Nessie.

"Of course not," Nessie agreed. But there was nothing agreeable about her tone.

She took a sip of tea, then went on.

"When Esther asked for a new life the witches told her that she was living it. That she had already asked for a new life, and been given it. This life, the one where Shulamit dies, was it."

Well wasn't that a clever trick. The skeptical expression on my face gave me away.

"Not a trick," Nessie said, as if she'd read my mind. She shook her head, and fixed me with cold eyes. "Because the witches took out a photo album and showed Esther —" she tapped her forefinger on the table, as if on a page—"the pictures of Esther's first life. She'd been Nat's wife, and a mother, but with just one child—a shy boy named Jonathan. He lived the life of a scholar. Never married.

"The witches showed Esther a letter she'd sent Jonathan on her 75th birthday. The poor man had asked her if there were anything she would have done differently if she could have lived her life over. She wrote back: 'I'd have had more children because you are such a disappointment.'

"Esther had gone to the Treyad at 75 and asked for a new life, with more children. And she had been given it."

I shivered. A cool breeze was sweeping up from the lake. I stood up and closed the kitchen window.

"Ellie, how do you suppose we know this?" came Nessie's voice from behind me.

Reluctantly, I turned. In the dark kitchen, Nessie's face was no longer old, but timeless. Beside her, Helen sat, uncharacteristically silent, eyes cast down at the knitting in her lap. Nessie watched me as I walked back to the table and sat down in my chair.

"You want me to believe that you two are witches?" I asked. Thinking if Harold finds out about this craziness, he's going to petition for guardianship and put them in the nursing home. "I mean, aren't there supposed to be three?"

Nessie and Helen just looked at me. Reba, I thought. Oh God.

"All that yarn in the cellar?" Nessie made a sound that might have been a laugh. "Those are from lives we've unraveled. You'd be surprised how many people still come to the Treyad for help. Not just the old people, either. People just like you."

I shook my head, appalled at the direction this was taking. "So, what, you think I need your help with Sarah?"

"Maybe." Helen's deep voice broke in. "But that's beside the point."

She paused, turning to her sister. "Nessie, we should have told Ellie earlier."

"I know. I know."

"Told me what?" I asked.

I put down my tea, now over-brewed and bitter.

"Told you," said Nessie. "Told you...Ellie, it's time for you to take Reba's place in the Treyad. You're a witch, an unraveler. You can change people's lives. You were born with that power, and we're going to show you how it works."

I sat stunned for a moment, then shrugged, hoping to shake off their words. The great-aunts were worse off than I'd thought.

"I don't want to be a witch," I tried to chuckle, but it came out as a nervous giggle. "Other people's lives? I've made a mess of my own life. I've made a mess of Sarah's. I don't want the responsibility."

"We'll teach you the skills," Nessie pushed on. "How to listen. How to advise. And the spells of transformation. How to set the time and date at which your client's life will spin off into another lifeline."

Her matter-of-fact tone made the patent craziness seem almost real.

"No," I said. "No, I'm sorry. I don't want any part of this."

Nessie's face turned dark. She slapped the table.

"Maybe it doesn't matter what you want, Ellie," she said. "I tell you, you were born to this. And with Reba gone, we need you."

I argued with them late into the night.

"I need to go back to the city," I told them.

"Fine. Go." Nessie stood up, turned her back on me, and headed down the hall toward her bedroom, leaving Helen and me alone at the table. Helen took a deep breath and clasped her hands, pausing as if for prayer. She mumbled a few words to herself before she spoke to me.

"Ellie, I remember the day my own great-aunts told the three of us that we would become a Treyad. So many years ago, in Kovno."

"How did you feel?"

"It was different then. It was..." Helen shook her head and smiled sadly. "I don't think you can imagine."

But she was wrong. With Nessie out of the room, I found it possible to imagine this old woman had magical powers.

"Can a witch change her own life?" I'd been wondering. "I mean, could I go back to the days when Sarah was young, and I was offered that job in California, and I could have left and made a new life for us. Could I send myself back?"

Helen shook her head and laughed. "No. You can't send yourself back."

I nodded. Well, no surprise.

Helen leaned close and whispered, "But I can."

She closed the wrinkled lids over her cloudy brown eyes for a moment. When she reopened them, her pupils were brighter and clear.

"We'll have to hurry," she said softly. "Nessie is set on you completing the Treyad. But..."

"I don't want to."

"I know." Helen got up and went to the old sideboard and quietly slid open a drawer. She came back, clutching a pair of yellowed ivory needles.

"Clasp your hands," she whispered. Then she reached over, smelling faintly of sandalwood, and put my clasped hands on my lap.

"*Blaybn nokh*. Stay still."

She held her needles above my hands, and began knitting. There was no yarn, but Helen's needles clicked, faster and faster. The room went dark and then I felt them, felt threads flowing out of my fingertips. There was the occasional flash of pain, a tug, as if the yarn had become knotted. Had I'd told Helen how far back I wanted to go? I tried to speak, but couldn't. Helen's needles clicked and my past flowed out from my fingers, spilling onto the floor.

The next morning at breakfast I kissed the old girls goodbye, ducking their invitation to have coffee and whole grain rolls with them. I figured I'd stop for a latte and a croissant in the village.

I paused on the broad front porch to enjoy the dramatic view down to the lakeshore. I ran my hand along the smooth finish of the new railing. With handicapped access, better lighting, and other updates, Nessie and Helen would be able to stay here for a few more years. After that, I'd have it as a vacation home. It was sound investment.

The new Lexus had been a good choice, too. The car's leather seats were pleasantly warm in the morning sunlight.

Before starting the car, I pulled my mobile phone from my bag and texted Doug to let him know I'd be just a few minutes late for lunch at our favorite Thai place in Westchester.

Driving down the hill toward the lake, I lowered the car windows and savored the soft breeze. I slowed as I drove past the beach. Kids in bright-colored bathing suits scampered along at the edge of the sun-dappled water, squealing with delight.

The shady roadway ahead went blurry as my eyes filled with tears.

There were times when I wished I'd had children.

K.G. Anderson grew up in a small beach town outside Boston, where the mothers and grandmothers told stories from the old country. She sees traces of magic everywhere, even in the Seattle technology community where she makes her living. Her short fiction has been published in numerous anthologies and magazines, including The Mammoth Book of Jack the Ripper Stories. Visit Karen at http:// writerway.com/fiction-by-k-g-anderson/

Blacktop Tar Cobra Charmer

Dale Carothers

Drape heard them coming from the west. Their carts had a westerly jangle, their donkeys a westerly bray.

He lifted the tarpaper that covered the west-facing window of his shack. Yup. There they were. Coming along in a ragged line. Slow and tired. Oppressed by the heavy sunlight that scorched the mid-country crossroads. Heat waves obscured their feet, and they appeared to walk on air with half formed legs.

The crossroads lay somewhere in the center of what used to be America. One spoke ran north-south, the other east-west, and Drape's shack stood in the northeast corner. Drape didn't know what state, but he thought it was one of those big ones, with all straight lines on its borders and right angles at its corners.

Drape smiled. If they needed directions, he'd get some food and quell the raging in his stomach.

He stripped down to his boxers, kicked off his flip-flops and went out. He squinted against the glare, and the crusty cancers that ridged his nose and cheeks began to itch.

The blacktop was faded, but still dark enough to absorb all kinds of sunlight. After an initial sizzle along his soles, the pain died down. He walked tightrope style along a stretched out blob of tar. It mushed up between his toes, but didn't stick.

Tar was the blood of the road: leaking out of its cracked flesh and forming scabs that softened in the heat. Drape reached out with his mind, feeling every road connected to this one. He knew who passed and when, knowing where they were going and why.

Drape waited. His back tightened as he soaked up the rays. His skin creaked like tape coming off the roll: a real slow cooking, taking years to turn him to jerky. Pain lanced across his skin in all directions, webbing like the roads on a map. He needed a new job. This one was killing him. He wished someone could spell him a while. Give him time to heal up. Maybe bring an end to the pain.

A lady broke off from the group. She was gray-haired, but she stood tall. The lines in her face ran deep with sweat and road dust. "You the Crossroads Man?"

"What do you think?"

She pursed her lips. "I ain't got time for bullshit."

"I'm The Man in the Middle. God of the Byways. The Cardinal of Directions."

"Cardinal, huh? Where's your pointy hat?"

Drape chuckled, dry and raspy. "At the cleaners."

She laughed too. The lines of her face tightened. Through her feet on the road, Drape saw the way she earned all those lines. Some good, some bad, and all of them in service of her life and her wisdom. He knew why she walked at the front of the pack.

"Ain't many of us left," she said. "And even though food is scarce, we're lonely. We want to join up with another pack."

"You got something to pay me with?"

She reached into her jacket, pulled something out and tossed it to Drape.

He caught it. Old wax paper wrapped around dried rabbit flesh. He sniffed it. A little gamey, but good enough. "Any water?"

The whole pack tensed. Several put their hands on their weapons.

"I'm only asking for a few drops," Drape said.

The gray-haired woman said, "Clean water is hard to come by. It's the new gold."

Some of the pack took aim to reinforce her point.

"There's no need to get all uppity," Drape said, raising his hands. "I guess I'll have to wait for the next rain."

The pack looked hopefully at the sky. It was so clear and so blue. Not a hint of a cloud in sight. The hope on their faces faded. But Drape's eyes saw farther. A deluge was two weeks out. It was long enough for many of them to forget that he'd said anything, but some of them would still give him credit.

"So," she said. "Where do we find others?"

"Not many left," Drape said.

"I know. But we were hoping…"

"Everybody off the road. I can't have you fouling up my reading."

The pack looked to the gray woman.

"Can we take turns cooling off in the shade?" she asked pointing to the shack.

"Nope." Drape jerked a thumb at the opposite corner. "Readings work best if you don't make me nervous by getting too near my stuff."

There wasn't anything of real value in Drape's shack. Just a few Mason jars he used to collect rain. He'd let people in some years ago and one of them had ripped the tarpaper over his south window, and no amount of tape cut out all the sunlight.

The pack filed off the road, leading their donkeys and pushing their carts to the southwestern corner of the crossroads.

Drape stood in the exact center of the crossroads. A two-foot blob of thick tar was framed by the narrow ends of the colored dashes left by two road crews long before the world was scorched by anger and hate. Yellow dashes ran north to south, and white dashes ran east to west.

Drape knelt, planting his calloused knees near the south end of the tar blob. Hot pain ground its way along the bones of his spine, and he ground what was left of his teeth just to keep things consistent. More often than not, he felt like he was pumping boiling crude instead of blood. When the pain ebbed, he raised his palms to the sun and then slapped them on the pavement on both sides of the blob.

"Houp, houp, houp gadou," he sang, slapping his palms beside the blob in a rapid rhythm and leaning forward and back so that his hands ran in a pattern on each side of it. "Houp, houp, houp gadou."

The blob bubbled and melted. Drape stopped his back and forth, and waved his hands like a man wafting smoke up from a fire. The blob stood, thinning into a line, and then expanding at its top like a cobra's hood.

Drape charmed the tar cobra with his song and with his hands. A mouth formed and Drape leaned in, the loose wattle under his chin shivering with anticipation. The cobra lashed out and sank its fangs into Drape's face. Drape fell. His back twisted awkwardly and his shoulder blades scraped against the road.

While he lay paralyzed, visions bloomed in his mind, and the cancers on his face grew.

When his fit was over, and he lay slack and let out a long breath, the gray-haired woman took out a worn, plastic bottle and let three drops of water fall onto his lips.

"More," Drape said, his tongue darting out to taste the water before the sun dried it away.

"That's all I can spare."

"One more drop won't kill you."

"And one more drop won't slake your thirst," she said putting the cap back on the bottle. "What did you see?"

Drape scowled at her, and got ready to snatch the bottle from her hand. But a stray sunray made a lens of the water and blinded him. He blinked, and didn't see where she stowed the bottle. Defeated and thirsty, he said, "South."

"So people are moving south, to the ocean?"

"Yes."

She helped Drape up, and led him to his shack.

"Thank you," she said. "I knew you'd be our salvation. We need more people to strengthen our pack, to make sure we have enough fertile youngsters to keep our family alive."

"Hurry on now. People move around a lot. You need to get there before they leave."

The gray woman smiled one more time before walking away. "Everybody! Off your asses and on the road! We need to get a move on!"

The pack turned their carts and steered their donkeys back onto the road. Atop one broken-down nag was a little girl. Her afro was divided into two puff-ball pigtails, and in the sun her hair looked more red than black. She even had a spray of freckles across her chocolate-brown nose.

———————————————————————

Twelve years later, Drape had his first repeat visitor. She came alone.

She still wore her hair in puff-ball pigtails. She'd grown, but not much. Even with the afro, she barely crested five feet. Worn army pants sagged from her hips, and her white t-shirt had gone gray. Yellow patches colored the armpits. Her backpack was tight against her shoulder blades and her blue sunglasses obscured half her face.

Drape let the tarpaper covering his southern window fall back into place and went out to meet her. He started unbuttoning his shirt.

"Don't bother getting undressed. I don't need directions." She put out her hand. "My name is Hynde."

"Drape," he said, shaking her hand.

"Do you remember me and mine?"

"Yup."

"Why'd you lie to us?" Hynde asked.

"I didn't lie, not exactly."

Hynde pulled the hem of her shirt up to reveal the pistol stuck in her waistband. "None of that sidestepping shit, now. This is one of those truth or trigger situations."

"It won't do you any good," Drape said, suppressing a laugh. It sounded like she'd rehearsed her tough talk, but he didn't want to push it. "You can't kill me."

"Why not?"

"If you pulled that pistol and shot the road, would it die?"

Hynde brushed the pistol with her fingertips. "No, but it'd leave a nasty scar."

"A scar worth coming all this way?"

Hynde looked down at her frayed combat boots, and, after a minute, let the hem of her shirt fall. "What did you mean 'not exactly'?"

"I didn't answer the question your leader asked, but instead the one she should've asked."

Hynde took off her sunglasses and hung them from her collar. The mirrored lenses looked like an over-large dollar store pendant. "I see." She took a few steps closer. "You gave us the answer we needed, and not the answer we wanted."

"Yeah."

"Didn't our loneliness mean anything to you?"

"Not as much as it meant to you."

"What do you mean?"

Drape sat cross-legged on the blacktop and Hynde followed suit.

"You came to me soon after your pack formed," Drape said. "You were a loose collection of people, not a family. Easily broken, if not given time to strengthen your bonds." Drape itched at the cancer on his nose. Black flakes of burned, diseased skin came off under his fingernail. He flicked it away. "And you did meet up with others eventually."

"Yeah, really 'eventually'. Like years and years."

"When you're as young as you are, years feel pretty long. That goes away with time. And it must've worked out for your pack. Otherwise you wouldn't have left them to come find me."

"I guess."

"It's my turn to ask a question."

Her face wrinkled up in concern. "Go ahead."

"Why did you come back?"

"I needed to know more about your...what you..." Hynde waved her hand in a circle.

"Who's lying now?"

Her mouth formed into a pout. "Am not."

"Nobody comes all that way just to learn how it all works. There ain't no use in it."

Hynde shrugged.

"How about you tell me the real reason you came?"

"Fine, I will." Hynde stood and paced, mumbling to herself.

While Drape watched the black soles of Hynde's boots press against the blacktop, he wondered if the road would ever get so hot that the soles would melt and become one with the road. "You any closer to an answer? My legs are getting stiff."

Hynde walked back and sat down. She fidgeted; crossing and uncrossing her legs.

"Whenever you're ready, sweetheart."

She tipped her head down and glared up at him. "I'll tell you if shut up, sweetheart."

Drape gave a dry chuckle.

Hynde put her sunglasses back on, like she wanted to hide from what she had to say.

"My pack is strong, but nowhere near strong enough. All of us got to do our part, making the pack grow. But…not me."

"Not me, what?"

Hynde let out a long breath. "I don't want to be a mother. I want something more. Something bigger."

Drape smiled. "Now we're getting somewhere."

"Why're you so happy? This ain't something to be happy about. I feel bad for betraying my pack. I've been told all my life. Fill my womb. Make the pack strong. Be fruitful. All that shit."

"And you think you're destined for something bigger?"

She slid her sunglasses down her nose. "I can feel it right down to the soles of my boots."

"That's a tall order. I'll need your help." He stood, stripped down to his boxers and knelt near the oblong tar blob. He pointed at the road. "Kneel down next to that little line of tar."

"Oh no, this is your thing. Not mine."

"If you want to learn about your thing you'll have to help me with mine." He hated lying to her, but he had a solution in mind. For both of them.

"If you say so." Hynde shimmied her backpack off her shoulders and then reached for her fly.

"Stop," Drape said. "You can keep your clothes on."

A look of relief crossed her face. "I don't mind-"

"Stripping down to my underwear is part of my process, but it doesn't have to be part of yours."

Hynde lowered herself to the road. "Okay."

"I'll set up the rhythm. You just follow along with me. We have to synchronize for this to work."

"Got it."

Drape started slapping the ground and chanting, "Houp, houp, houp gadou."

"Wait a minute."

Drape stopped. "What?"

"Your tar thingy is way bigger than mine."

"There's no reason to get tar blob envy here. A bigger blob means a bigger snake and a bigger dose of poison. You need to start small."

"I'm strong, I can take it. Don't you dare—" Hynde flinched and sat back. "Wait. Did you say poison?"

"Seers, shamans, and such have been using poisons to summon visions for hundreds of years. Ain't no real harm in it. Unless you do it for years on end. Then there's side effects." He pointed to his face.

Hynde stood. "I don't know about this."

"Don't you want the answer to your question?"

"Yeah."

"This is how you get it."

Hynde took a step toward her backpack and nudged it with her toe.

Drape grabbed his pants and made like he was getting up. "Looks like I was wrong. You ain't strong enough for something bigger. Go back to your tribe and start pushing out babies."

Hynde scowled and dropped to her knees, framing the little tar blob. "Let's do this."

"You sure? You look like you'd make a good mommy."

Hynde leaned down and put her hands on the blacktop.

Drape dropped his pants and got in position.

They slapped and chanted. It took her a minute to match his rhythm, but once she did, she fell into the trance along with him. Drape waved his hands upward, summoning the cobra. The tar bubbled and rose, forming into the hooded snake. Her little blob rose too, but didn't form into a cobra, though its little tail formed a rattle that shook in time with their ritual.

Both snakes opened their mouths to reveal dripping fangs. They struck in unison. Drape and Hynde fell limp to the blacktop.

Drape waited for Hynde to adjust to the differences in the world. He'd grown used to the altered colors, the muted—but still bright—sunlight. Everything had shifted and taken on a more lively focus, like a world seen through amber-colored lenses.

"Wow," Hynde said. "I never knew…It's just so…" She waved her hand at the world around them.

"Yeah," Drape said. "It is."

The road pulsed beneath their feet, alive with the stories of the thousands who'd passed. Beginnings, destinations, detours and sudden violent ends.

"Since you asked, I guess I'll tell you how it all works," Drape said. "Road signs don't mean anything because the names of the places they lead to don't mean anything, not anymore."

"I don't get it."

Drape stood in the middle of the crossroads. He pointed in each direction in turn. "Minneapolis, Los Angeles, Dallas and New York don't mean anything anymore. They aren't real destinations anymore. North, south, east and west still have meaning, but only in terms of weather and landscape."

"All those places are still there. I've been to L.A."

"I know, but it's not L.A. anymore. Not in the way it used to be."

"But that's true everywhere. Everything changes over time."

"You've likely seen some changes, the slow advances of what seemed to be new, but was just humankind regaining things we had before the Infestation."

Drape had been a long haul trucker, Before. He never had a home, other than his sleeper cab and the varied hotels and motels along his routes. He worked the entire country, signing on with several different companies so he could get to know every strip of road.

But then the spores came—small as a baby's toe, glowing turquoise, ciliated—and swirled in vast eddies from the outer atmosphere all the way to the ground. They scorched entire continents and dried up vast areas of oceans. Millions died, but some survived. And when the spores faded, they left strange pockets of animism all over the world. Like Drape and his connection to the roads.

"Momma used to tell me stories," Hynde said. "The old world is hard for me to understand. I never got to see it."

"Then why do the old world and its ways matter?"

"The elders of the pack always talked about it. About how good it was, and how we had to get back to the way things were before. I guess I'm just clinging to their memories."

"It's that connection to the old ways that scares me. That's why I send people where they need to go, instead of where they think they want to go." Drape spun, waving a hand at the roads. "These roads used to lead to cities, but now they lead to Happiness, Despair, Life, Death, Loss, and Gain. It changes all the time, depending on the people who go there and how they live when they get there."

"What's all this got to do with my wanting a bigger purpose in life?"

"I'll get to that. Just tell me if you see what I mean."

"I see."

Drape looked into Hynde's eyes, and saw that she did, in fact, see.

"I was hoping you'd say that." Drape moved in close and put his hands on her shoulders. "I need you to take over for me."

"I can't. My pack needs me."

"You left them behind so you could come here and ask me for a new purpose."

"But how does that answer my question?"

"In the best way possible." Drape smiled and patted her shoulder. "I've been waiting for someone like you. Someone to take the pain away. Someone brave enough to let the snake bite them."

Hynde looked at the twin marks on her hand. Flakes of crusted black cancer had already formed around the wound. She punched Drape and he fell to the road. "Fucker! What did you do to me?"

"I gave you what you wanted," Drape said. Blood and tar dripped from his nose. "The cancer is eating away at my body, and I needed someone to replace me."

She kicked him in the leg. "You tricked me."

"I made you something bigger," Drape said, hissing in pain. A black bruise formed on his thigh. "Something powerful."

"But now I'm stuck here."

"You asked for it. I gave it to you." Drape shivered, and his skin cracked open. Cancer formed at the broken edges of his skin and crept along, absorbing the healthy flesh. Tar oozed from his wounds. "There's no going back now. You need to accept it."

Hynde knelt next to him. "I'm afraid."

"So was I, when the power came over me." Drape raised a melting hand and grabbed Hynde's arm. "You were strong enough to survive this world, and strong enough to get back here on your own. You're strong enough for this."

"Really?"

Hope was the last thing he could give her. "Yeah."

Tar flowed up Hynde's hand and under the cuff of her sleeve. She screamed as it gushed into her mouth, and her scream turned to a gargle of tarry bubbles.

"The blood of the road belongs to you now," Drape said. "As it flows through your veins, so too, it flows along the highways and byways of what used to be America. Learn the stories of the people and weave them together into a whole, so that they survive what's been done to the world."

What was left of Drape melted, and seeped into the cracks in the blacktop. He leached into the soil below and continued on downward.

Deep within the Earth, Drape collected in a narrow fissure, and then ran down a fat stalactite, dripping off its point into a vast underground lake of tar.

His sense of self faded until he was little more than a dreaming, lamellar flow, sliding over, under and between other pockets of effluvia.

Life and thought came back to him only when he crossed over cracks that opened onto the burning core of the Earth. In those moments he rose in burning bubbles and flashed into flames on the surface of the tar.

In those brief instants of light and insight he wondered how Hynde fared on the surface.

Dale Carothers lives in Minnesota with his wife, Sara, and an emotionally demanding beagle. He provides independent living skills training for adults with disabilities and eats way more cake than he should. Find links to his work and leave a comment at dalecarothers.wordpress.com.

The Silk Silvered Skulls of Millen Mir

James Van Pelt

"Nothing beats a great book," said Les Bullard. He waited below Miss Rhonim as she stood on the ladder, searching the upper shelf. Remarkably fit for a librarian. Solid upper arms, well muscled legs. A statuesque Amazonian in black-framed glasses. She fit in with the library's décor, which leaned toward medieval armaments.

"You know you read the title when you were young?"

"Fifth grade or maybe sixth. I went through a long heroic fantasy phase. Tarzan and Conan and John Carter and Elric of Melniboné. The eternal champions. I wanted to be Doc Savage. God, I loved those books."

"This one, though, it wasn't part of a series?" She pulled on the shelf to move the ladder a couple feet.

"Nope. Just one, medium-sized book. Mine had a red leather cover and gold-edged pages. Nicest book I ever carried in my backpack. A maroon ribbon sewn into the binding to mark my spot."

"But you don't know the author?"

Les wrinkled his brow. "I can tell you how the book smelled. I can tell you what it was like to lay on my grandmother's freezer in her cellar during sweltering, summer Ohio days, reading the book by the light of the open door. I can tell you about starting the book after breakfast, and reading until it grew dark. I walked from the cellar up a little flight of stairs and into her backyard where fireflies winked over the vegetable patch. But I can't recall the author's name. It was three words, I think, like Jaime Fitz Mason or Robin Trait Curran. Something with that rhythm."

"I can't do a search for an author's name by rhythm."

"Maybe I'm misremembering the title." But Les was sure he wasn't. He closed his eyes and saw the book in the cellar's dimness, could feel the weight in his hand. Black letters embossed on red leather with a silver vine woven through them: *The Silk Silvered Skulls of Millen Mir*. He loved the opening line: "The swordsman's horse carried the weary warrior down a stony path."

Miss Rhonim ran her finger across the books' spines, one after another. "You came to the right place for hard to find books. The Orne Library at Miskatonic University is world-renowned."

Les looked down the long, poorly lit shelves. Small fluorescent fixtures hung from the ceiling at ten-foot intervals, but only the lights within fifteen feet of them were on. Darkness shrouded the rest. The cement floor reflected nothing. He couldn't see the wall at either end. "I heard your library had the best collection of uncataloged titles in North America. I've been looking for this book for decades."

"That's dedication. Heroic fantasy, fairly contemporary language, you said?"

"I didn't have trouble reading it when I was twelve, but I read well above grade level. I finished *All Quiet on the Western Front* the next year. Most depressing book of all time. I swore off fine literature for years after that."

"So probably written in the late 1800s but no later than 1965 or so. We're in the right section, but we have thousands of titles, as you can see. It might take a bit." She glanced at her watch. "This is the restricted collection. There are irreplaceable texts stored down here. One of a kind. Patrons have to be accompanied."

Les bent to inspect the bottom row. His back creaked. "Why aren't these titles in a database? How do you find anything?"

She stiffened. "The Orne Library is the largest gathering of rare and historic texts in the northern hemisphere. In the general collection there are several million titles. Only Harvard contains more works than we do. Our Pickman Archive holds the finest examples of early Americana in the world, including settler diaries, journals and ledgers. We have letters from the original pilgrims. I think we do very well considering the complexity of our collection."

"I wasn't criticizing."

Miss Rhonim continued scanning book titles, clearly taking a few calming breaths. "Sorry to sound defensive, but you don't have to work in the Orne long before you realize the value of these books. Besides, the deeper collection is... difficult."

"What do you mean?"

"The books aren't always where we leave them. They... um... rearrange. Like this..." She held a black volume in her hand, "... is from 1788. It's misplaced. The faculty has learned to take a book when they find it. It might not be there again."

"So my title could be anywhere?" When they'd come down the long, stone stairway to this level, Les had thought they were going to a reading room or display area, but what greeted them at the bottom was a corridor formed by the ends of bookshelves that reached ceiling to floor. The lights must have been attached to motion sensors because they turned on as the two approached and blinked out behind them. At each junction, more neatly shelved books greeted him, row after row, until he lost count. They made several turns to reach the area they were in now, and not all were right angles. Some books stood in large circular shelves, like roundabouts, and others were stored in triangular formations, twenty feet to a side. Periodically they came upon a chair with an attached writing surface or a study table, but he hadn't seen another person. "I'm not surprised you lose books. The way this place is built, you could lose librarians."

"If your book exists, we have it. Looking is the only way to uncover anything; the loose organization down here is a feature, not a bug. The restricted collection is less about finding and more about discovering, Mr. Bullard. Our researchers and the books they need eventually cross paths." She replaced a book firmly on the shelf. "Imagine coming down here in the 1800s when you would have been holding a lantern."

The idea made him shiver.

They searched for another hour, Miss Rhonim using the ladder for the high shelves, and Les reading the low ones. He examined beautiful books, some with illustrated covers. One showed a burly savage wrestling an alligator, jaws open and stretching back, trying to kill the muscular human. Broken pillars like a coliseum's remains stood in the misty background. He liked the style, but the artist was unfamiliar. "Can I check this out?"

Miss Rhonim nodded. "Twenty-four hours only. You have to sign a waiver and leave a deposit."

That night, Les made himself comfortable on the motel bed, turned on the reading light, then opened the book, *A Jungle Crown at Katung Pass* by Sideon Wayte. It had a faded inscription in pencil he hadn't noticed before: "To Beatrice, my jungle queen. Raymond, Christmas, 1908." So, written before Burroughs published *Tarzan.*

Twenty minutes into the book, Les climbed from the bed to stretch his back. When he'd retired two years ago, he'd looked forward to long periods of uninterrupted reading—a return to his youth. But now he couldn't stay in one posture more than thirty minutes before his back or neck hurt. Even holding the book made his elbows and fingers ache. He wondered if arthritis might be kicking in. And he could never find quite the right position for his bifocals. He kept adjusting his head to focus properly.

In junior high, he carried at least a couple novels in his backpack, waiting for class to begin so he could sneak one out. Mr. Crutcher, his 8th grade history teacher, would turn his back to write on the board, and Les would have his book open. Then, like the snap of his fingers, class ended. For forty minutes, the teacher and his lesson faded away. When the bell rang, Les had to shake himself back to reality. He walked the halls in bewilderment because the literary world felt so much more real than the school. By the end of the day, he would have finished the book and started another. He read at night, long after he was supposed to be asleep, so he could reach the new book's end.

Reading connected him to his youth. He didn't have to be able to run and jump like a fifteen year old if he could read like one.

Les sat on the bed's edge, reopened the book. The story wasn't bad, even if the language stumbled in places. Sideon Wayte couldn't turn a phrase, but he wrote with a cheerful, testosterone-soaked cheesiness. The villain was particularly black-hearted, the jungle animals "snarled with wild ferocity" and the women were slender, "small-handed" creatures who swooned on cue. In other words, *A Jungle Crown at Katung Pass* was a book of its time. It certainly didn't measure up to *The Silk Silvered Skulls of Millen Mir*.

If he could just find the book again! His gnawing obsession. For years he'd haunted used bookstores and antique shops, hoping he'd spot the familiar red cover. The summer at grandma's house in Ohio, that had been his only title. He couldn't remember where he got it. Maybe he'd found it in her living room bookcase where she kept a collection of Reader's Digest condensed classics along with a few others. Surely his parents hadn't given it to him. They favored cheap paperbacks.

He'd always been a fast reader. Other books he finished in a day (even the fat and deeply depressing *All Quiet on the Western Front*), but he started *The Silk Silvered Skulls* when he arrived at Grandma's. He read every day for hours. He read after dinner and deep into the night, but he never finished the book. His memory of that summer was of delirious hours lost in Millen Mir. It seemed as if he was always in the middle, more pages to go, and he loved it. Other books passed too fast until the sad dread of knowing only a few pages remained crept up on him. The dream would soon end. He'd turn the final page where the text didn't reach the bottom and the facing page was blank. *Lord of the Rings* lasted three days in the 9th grade. He didn't sleep. He faked a cough so he could skip school when he reached *The*

Return of the King. Mom left him in his room, Mentholatum rubbed into his chest, vaporizer bubbling, buried in his blankets, deep in Middle Earth. The remaining pages grew fewer and fewer. Sweat poured from him as he lingered over the final paragraphs. The last pages wrinkled in the humid room until he finished, totally drained, sorry the book didn't go on.

But not *The Silk Silvered Skulls of Millen Mir.* How was it possible that he read just that one book all summer? Did he finish, and then lost in the book's spell, turn back to the beginning to start again?

Les put a pillow under his knees. Maybe if he could find just the right position, he would disappear into *A Jungle Crown at Katung Pass* like he did when he was young. He could capture the timelessness again, the dreamy creaminess of pages that vanished, of words that turned into worlds? But the pages remained stubbornly opaque. He tried squinting, turning the light down, relaxing breaths. How did he do it when he was a schoolboy? What was the secret?

After shifting position a dozen times, stretching his back twice, and drinking two cups of strong coffee, Les finished *A Jungle Crown at Katung Pass* after midnight. The story wasn't bad, but he didn't magically transport into it either. He rested the book on his chest and listened to cars on the highway whipping past the motel. The clock on the nightstand ticked loudly, and through the thin walls, a couple argued.

When he slept, he dreamed of the ruins of Millen Mir, of dread creatures that rose from catacombs at night, of a magnificent barbarian king camped among the moss covered walls, his back to the fire, holding back black spirits through strength of will.

Miss Rhonim met him at the double doors that lead into the Orne. She wore a brown blazer over a white blouse and mid-calf skirt. In the morning light that bathed the library's front, she looked more like a Valkyrie than a librarian. He wondered if she worked out. Les carried a small backpack. He thought it made him more like a student, albeit an elderly one. The doors closed behind them, shrouding the library's lobby in twilight silence. Real students sat in study carrels, reading by small lights mounted on goosenecks.

"I believe I have a lead on your book, Mr. Bullard. We searched fiction, but what if it was shelved as history or biography? We're going to different sections today."

The stairs to the deeper stacks loomed even darker than they had earlier. Miss Rhonim unlocked the gate and pushed it aside. Lights flicked on as they descended.

"This seems like more stairs than yesterday," said Les. He didn't climb as well as ten years ago, and the trip back become more intimidating the farther they walked.

"That's because it is. History is further down."

Swords in a long line hung from the wall to their right. Spears and shields on the left. Les touched a sword blade, moving the metal against the stone. It rang like a tiny bell. "Why all the armor?"

Miss Rhonim laughed. "Practicality. You never know when you might need a good sword. Besides, I thought you liked heroic fantasy. This should be a dream come true for you."

Like yesterday, the path into the books confused Les. Not only were many of the turns at odd angles, the floor sloped in places so they walked down or up book-lined hills. Lights turned on as they approached and turned off where they'd been. Darkness faced them and followed.

"How deep does the library go?"

"A long way." Miss Rhonim stopped in front of a stack of books that looked indistinguishable from the ones they'd already passed. None were marked with bar codes or labels. Some were titled on the spine, but many were not. "We're in the right place if your book is in history. Biography is a bit of a walk from here." She climbed a ladder. "You know the routine."

"I brought these." He pulled a pair of gardening kneepads from his backpack. "I have a couple water bottles too if you want one. I didn't notice drinking fountains yesterday. Are we going to the left or right?"

"To the left. If your title is here, it will be within this thirty feet."

Les put the kneepads on over his khakis. His knees wouldn't take the same beating as the day before when he'd spent too much time on the cold cement. He knelt to search the lowest row. Books without titles had to be slid off the shelf. Some didn't have titles on the cover either, so Les fell into a routine of reaching in, slipping the book out, checking the title page, then carefully returning it. He remembered summer days in his library at home when he'd been a boy, sitting on the floor before the books. If his mom didn't expect him home, he would finish one, put it back in its place and then read the next. When he finally stood, he'd realize that he'd skipped lunch, and it would be time to ride his bike home for dinner.

Methodically, Les checked each book. Miss Rhonim showed him where to stop and to start with the higher shelf. He paused with some, marveling at their illustrations, repulsed by others. Hand-written inscriptions in spidery calligraphy marked the inside covers, most dated from the early 1900s to 1940.

A metallic clank sounded from the darkness beyond, distinct, sharp and sudden. Miss Rhonim paused, a book in hand, preternaturally alert.

"What was that?"

"Hush," she said. "I'll check it out. You keep looking."

She climbed down the ladder noiselessly, took off her shoes, put them neatly under the ladder, then moved toward the sound, partly crouched, lithe as a cat. Ceiling lights turned on in front of her until she walked with an island of her own light. She turned down a row a hundred feet away, and suddenly Les felt naked and alone. If she didn't come back, he didn't know the way out, but worse than that was the darkness lurking beyond the fifteen feet of light to his left and right. He could almost see large things standing silently, studying him. Les's knees cracked when he stood.

Cautiously, he walked in the direction opposite the one Miss Rhonim had taken. A ceiling light flicked on, not revealing monsters, but more books. He laughed to himself. The lights were the secret. They were motion activated, so creatures trying to sneak up on him would trigger a light and show themselves. They were the library's early warning system, but his self-assurances felt hollow. He looked back to where his backpack now sat on the edge of light. Another step or two, and it too would be lost in the dark.

"Miss Rhonim," he called. "Are you okay?" The sound faded without echo or answer. He turned his head to the side, quieted his breath. Somewhere, metal met metal, just on perception's edge. Was that a shout? Was that a roar? He ran past his backpack, following Miss Rhonim, but when he reached an intersection he stopped, gasping for breath and unsure where to go. His heart pounding obscured sounds. "Miss Rhonim! Miss Rhonim!"

Away in the darkness, a ceiling light flicked on. The librarian strode toward him.

"You really shouldn't wander in here," she said when she drew close. "It can be a bit of a maze."

"What was it? I thought I heard something."

"Nothing to worry about. A maintenance issue, really. Why don't we see if we can't find your book now."

She led him back to the shelves they'd been searching.

It wasn't until Miss Rhonim climbed the ladder again that Les noticed a rip in her blazer and blouse, a foot-long cut on her left side angling down from her armpit and ending below her shoulder blade. Les knelt, looking up at her. Not a rip so much as a clean cut like from a knife or sword. Her skin was untouched beneath. He was sure her clothes weren't damaged earlier. What happened to her when she left?

He tried to figure out how to ask her about it, but the next book he pulled from the shelf drove the question from him. Red cover. Black embossed title with a silver vine running through the letters.

"Oh, god," he said, and sat back. *The Silk Silvered Skulls of Millen Mir*, as beautiful as he remembered, by Danny Jan Milton.

"You found it?" Miss Rhonim sounded delighted as she climbed down the ladder. She crouched beside him. "May I?"

She hefted the book in her hand, opened it. "Ah, I see why you thought it was special. Not many like this one."

"What do you mean?"

Miss Rhonim said, "Have you ever gone into an elementary school library?"

Les nodded.

"Most have a sign somewhere, often by the entrance, or a bulletin board. It says, 'Books: Your Ticket to Adventure.'"

Les did remember exactly those words in his childhood library, accompanied with rockets and unicorns and castles. He thought it was true then just as he did now.

Miss Rhonim handed the book back. "Some books don't take you as far, but some, like yours, are infinity passes. I can tell just by holding it. This is a valuable book indeed, exceptionally rare."

Tears burned on Les's cheeks. He'd searched so long. "Can I... check it out?"

Miss Rhonim shook her head. Crouched beside him, her face so close, Les noticed her eyes for the first time, sword-metal grey with copper flecks. Startling at this distance, intense but not unkind.

Les pulled the book to his chest. "I can't?"

"Here's why." She held her hand out.

Reluctantly, Les gave it back.

The librarian opened the front cover and showed it to him. "I believe it's your book."

In familiar handwriting, the inscription read, "To Les, my little reader, from Grandma."

"How?"

Miss Rhonim straightened, towering over him. "I told you. Down in the Orne's deep stacks, you and the book you need eventually cross paths. It's one of our best features."

"I can keep it?" He ran his hand over the lettering. The leather felt warm, as if the book had a life of its own. He knew that when he opened it, when he read, it would be as if he was fifteen again. He remembered landscapes that caressed his senses, fogs that chilled his face, forest meadows filled with pine and sweet grass scents, rivers clapping over rounded boulders, the long road and his companions waiting on rampart walls. Not just a ticket, but a key and a pass and a secret handshake into his childhood imagination.

Miss Rhonim turned her gaze from him, peered into the darkness beyond. Her posture alerted Les. He looked back, trying to see what she detected.

"Time to go," she said as she helped him to his feet with one hand and scooped up his backpack with the other.

Beyond the ceiling light's reach, a shuffling sound, a click like bone against stone, or claws.

"We'll be moving smartly here," she said, not flustered, but concentrated and competent. "Looks like I didn't quite solve the problem earlier."

She kept one hand on his elbow, guiding him through the book maze back toward the stairs to the main library.

"If something's following us, why don't the lights turn on?" Les kept checking over his shoulder. There was never more than fifteen feet illuminated behind him. Fifteen feet would only be three or four strides for someone, or something, running, and clearly they were being trailed. If a shape appeared, he would have no time to react.

The librarian turned at a junction, almost jerking him off his feet. "We're visitors. They're denizens. Visitors need light. Denizens don't."

Confused, Les was nearly running to keep up with her. "Do we need to get help? Are they trespassers?" But even as he asked, he thought the question ridiculous. Whatever was going on here didn't feel like a job for the police. It was like he'd stepped into one of his books. If he'd been by himself, he would have been scared, but Miss Rhonim pushed him differently. Not frightened at all. Not out of her element.

The next turn took them to the stairs.

"This is where I leave you," she said. "Just keep going up until you get to the gate." She handed him a large key. "Lock it behind you."

"How will you get out?"

The librarian stepped to the wall, took down a sword and swung it once as if she'd done it thousands of times before. "Oh, there's more ways out than the stairs."

She put her hand on his shoulder. "You're a kindred spirit, Les. I hope you enjoy your book. Now, off you go."

Propelled by her last push, Les climbed several steps. He stopped to watch her stride back into the library, sword tip up and at the ready. She rounded a corner out of sight, and the lights that followed her flicked off. Then, a yell of triumph, the hard clatter of sword on sword, a guttural yell.

Les fled up the stairs, thankful Miss Rhonim took up the battle behind. She felt like she'd stepped from the land of Millen Mir. He'd been in the presence of a hero.

Carefully, after the long, long climb, Les locked the gate as she'd directed. He found a study carrel by the front door, clicked on a reading light and put the book on the wood desk. He'd read until she returned, not that he doubted she would. No, he didn't doubt that Miss Rhonim the librarian would return.

He settled into the chair, took a deep breath, opened the book to chapter one. The pages welcomed his fingers. He'd come home again. By the end of the first sentence, the letters weren't words on the page; they were a voice in his ear and a picture in his head.

"The swordsman's horse carried the weary warrior down a stony path."

A former high school English teacher, James Van Pelt writes full time in western Colorado. His fiction has made numerous appearances in most of the major science fiction and fantasy magazines. He has been a finalist for a Nebula Award, the Colorado Blue Spruce Young Adult Book Award, and been reprinted in many year's best collections. His first novel, Summer of the Apocalypse, *was released in 2006. His third collection of stories,* The Radio Magician and Other Stories, *received the Colorado Book Award in 2010. His latest collection,* Flying in the Heart of the Lafayette Escadrille, *was released in October of 2012. His new young adult novel,* Pandora's Gun *was released at the Spokane Worldcon.*

DRIVING DIRECTIONS

DAVID SKLAR

Dig straight down until you find a gate in a cavern wall beside a subterranean river that smells like blood. Drive through the gate and down the spiral stairs.

Under the stairs, drive across a plaza, and a field where stones jut up like crooked teeth. Drive until your car will go no more. Leave the car where it breaks down, leave it there, but take one tire, one hubcap, and one headlight.

One headlight will be dark. It will have forgotten how to burn. The other will still know what it is for, even when you have removed it from the car. Take this one, and use it to light your way.

In time you will come to a river underground. This river will have a different smell—of phosphorus, clay, and bone.

Wait for the boat.

When the ferryman asks for your fare, give him the hubcap. He will think you a wealthy traveler, because your coin is so large.

When you are halfway across the river, put the tire around your waist, and jump off. Hold the glowing headlight under the water, to scare off the eels. Or distract them. But if you do not have the lantern, your feet will be nipped to the bone.

Ride the current downstream until you see a limestone cliff carved out so it looks like a palace wall.

Swim toward the shore. You will overshoot. Be prepared to walk back through the shallows, over rocks and reeds and sticks, holding the headlamp low to protect you from eels and leeches. The light will be dimmer now, and the headlamp filled with water that faintly glows.

When you get to the cliffside palace, the doors will be locked. In glowing water poured from your sodden lamp, write "LET ME IN" on the ground before the doors. When the water is all poured out, your lamp will be dark.

If the gates do not open, you should have expected this. Walk home. If they open, walk into the dark.

David Sklar grew up in Michigan, where the Michipeshu nibbled his toes when Lake Superior was feeling frisky. A Rhysling nominee and a past winner of the Julia Moore Award for Bad Verse, David has more than 100 published works, including fiction in Strange Horizons, Daily Science Fiction, *and two previous* Triangulation *anthologies, as well as poetry in* Stone Telling *and* Ladybug, *and humor in* Knights of The Dinner Table *and* McSweeney's Internet Tendency. *David lives in New Jersey with his wife, their two barbarians, and a secondhand familiar, and he almost supports them as a freelance writer and editor.*

THE EVENING PATH

JENNIFER HYKES

"Never leave by the evening path," Grandmother said. "Leave always by the morning path, return by the morning path, and you will be safe." She said this often at night to Elise, shaking her pipe for emphasis, shrouding herself in smoke. Eyeing the window with narrowed eyes.

On the other side of the shuttered window, the evening paths glowed in the moonlight, silver strands snaking off into the woods and gods-knew-where. "Yes, grandmother," she said, every time.

Elise's mother broke that rule often, every time someone came with money and told her to. They came always with hard coin—credit was no use to them this far out at the edge of the kingdom—and a commission. That was what Mother always called it, "the commission," though it took many forms. Sometimes it was a finely-scribed letter in an envelope sealed with wax, sometimes it was a ragged scroll tied up in twine. Once, the commission had been transcribed in crude, uneven letters on a scrap of parchment, signed with a mark by a village elder who could not read, and handed over with reverence (and coin) by his deputy.

Mother read the commissions, counted out the coins, signed her name. Sometimes she bargained for more money. (Not in the beginning, not when she had been happy with whatever money they had been willing to give her, back when Elise was small and hungry and still thought that Father would return any moment from the hunt. But later, when Elise had grown softer and her mother sharper, sometimes she bargained.)

And when everything was done, the reading and the bargaining and the counting out of the coins and the signing, her mother left by the evening path.

The messenger always stayed, eating Mother's supper in her place. Grandmother sat frigid and silent in her chair, clutching her pipe with her good left hand and glaring at their guest.

"It's a bad business," she would tell Elise afterward, sitting in her chair close by the hearth. "Bad business, my little sparrow. Even the mills would be better."

"Yes, grandmother," she said, eyeing the twisted fingers of her grandmother's right hand.

"Get you off to bed now, and keep your window shut."

"Yes, grandmother," she said, though they both knew she would disobey.

The little round window above her attic bed looked out onto the meadow, where the evening paths wove through the tall grass towards the woods. They shimmered like streams of clear water in the moonlight, and if the night was still enough, they sang to her, a soothing hum in the back of her skull.

Only a few short steps past the treeline, the paths vanished completely. Into the evening woods, which lurked like a dark shadow behind the world she knew.

She never saw her mother cross over. But she knew her mother was there, somewhere in the woods, hunting. Elise always fell asleep long before Mother returned, but she woke at the sound of chain mail clinking in the crisp dawn air. There was Mother walking along the fading evening path between the woods and their cottage, her pike bobbing over her head, some dark thing slung over her shoulder. Sometimes it was just the head, all teeth and eyes and inky fur, unidentifiable by Elise but clearly wrong. But sometimes it was the whole carcass, enough for a week of eating. Despite the too-many eyes and too-long teeth, the creatures of the evening woods bore a meat sweeter and more succulent than any gamey thing trapped in the light of the morning woods.

Mother always came home just as the evening paths flickered out behind her and the morning paths began to glow golden in the meadow grass. Grandmother would scold her later for cutting it close, telling the same stories over and over about people lost forever to the evening woods when the paths vanished at dawn. But Elise never worried. Mother was wiser and more clever than all those silly people.

Mother looked up and met her watchful eyes with a proud and weary smile, and hoisted the monster she had slain.

Grandmother was up by then, and striking the ceiling with the butt of a broom handle. "Elise, my little sparrow, it's morning! Get you down here, my lazy bird, and help me with breakfast!"

Elise silently closed the window shutters. "Yes, Grandmother," she called, every time.

Another messenger had arrived. Elise, running home through the blue dusk, knew this long before she reached the front door. She could smell the sharp musk of the horse's sweat mixed with the faint perfume of some sweet herb she could not name. It lingered by a fading morning path, and pooled by the barn. She crossed the yard, following the trail. Her bare feet sent insects leaping from the cooling meadow grass.

She slid open the barn door. The horse lifted its head at her arrival. It was taller than any horse she had ever seen, and white as winter. Its mane was tied tightly up in ribboned bundles, and its body was sleek and well-fed. A surcoat checked in green and white lay neatly folded next to a fine-tooled saddle. The trappings hung on the wall, glinting with silver.

In the stillness, she heard the rush of its blood like a faraway river. She heard the stumbling beat of its heart.

Something was wrong with its heart.

A breeze blew in at her back. The horse tossed its head and shifted its weight, hoof to hoof and back again; its stumbling heart began to hurry. Elise slowed, frowning. It smelled the predator in her.

But she had no desire to harm it. "Hello," she whispered, setting a hand gently on its neck. It snorted once, and settled. Through the touch of its smooth hide, she felt the shift of layers of muscles, the shallow blood-courses and the deeper ones below that. And beating behind it all, a heart with a hole in it. She sighed through her nose, and the horse, perhaps in understanding, did the same. Broken bones she could set, torn flesh she could sew shut, but this was outside her skill. The best thing would be to put it to pasture, and let it live out its final days in peace. Giving the horse one final stroke on its long white nose, she shut the barn door and went inside, bits of grass still clinging to her toes.

The messenger was tall, like his horse, and almost as pale. His doublet was made of some soft, fine, deep-green fabric she could not name, and the cuffs of his shirt were trimmed in lace. He glanced at Elise when she entered, then turned his calm gaze back on her mother. He handed over the commission, an envelope sealed with a fat dollop of green wax imprinted with a single four-pointed star. He smelled like flowers.

"I did not know the duke was even aware of my humble operation," Mother said, taking the envelope.

The man did not smile. "The duke is quite aware of anything worth knowing about his lands." He tilted his head, as if Mother were some curious creature he was examining. "Such as, for example, a hunter's widow taking up his trade, and becoming surprisingly effective at it." Without waiting for an invitation, he sat down on Grandmother's chair by the fire. It was the nicest chair they had, all worn damask and solid oak legs, a wedding gift Grandmother had received in her maidenhood. Elise was not allowed to sit there, and Mother never did. Grandmother, who had stood at his arrival, bit back her complaint and sat down, wordless, at the table.

Mother popped the seal and unfolded the letter. Grandmother glanced down in disapproval at Elise's feet, and gestured sharply at the seat next to her, as if to say, *we will discuss what happened to your boots later.*

It was a long letter, and Mother made no movement while she read. At last she set the letter down on the table, lifted her chin and said, "Old Bonecrack."

Neither Elise nor her grandmother reached for the letter. Grandmother could not read; Elise could, but she felt a power in the name her mother spoke, and it made her feel small and ill. She did not want to touch the letter that bore such a name.

"Correct," said the messenger. "As you can see, the duke is willing to pay quite generously."

"Old Bonecrack?" Grandmother spat out the name. "Daughter, don't you be a fool!"

"The duke offers twelve hundred crowns for the head," said the messenger, projecting his voice without seeming to yell, "plus an annuity of fifty crowns. Enough to buy this land, with enough left over to keep you and your family quite comfortable for the rest of your days."

The messenger's heart beat fast and forceful, pounding in Elise's ears. But Mother's heart was unhurried: the heart of someone whose mind was already made up. Grandmother must have realized this too, though she had no sharpened hearing, for she pushed herself to her feet with a suddenness that belied her aging, aching bones. She took Mother by the arm and led her outside, shutting the door and leaving Elise inside with the messenger.

Elise couldn't hear what they said to one another. Her sharp hearing didn't work as sharply if she couldn't see what she was listening to. All she heard were voices rising in great rushes of sound, like the winds that blew through the forest right before a storm.

The messenger sat watching the fire, his fingers interlocked across the flat plane of his stomach. Firelight glinted off the line of gilded buttons that ran down the front of his doublet. Elise got a rag and began to clean the grass and dirt off her feet. The noise outside, and the quiet inside, unnerved her. She thought of telling the messenger about his horse, but Grandmother had warned her not to show strangers that she could do such things as hear the beating of their hearts.

"Who's Old Bonecrack?" she asked instead.

The messenger looked at her as if seeing her for the first time. "You've never heard of him? Well, I expect not, living as far out as you do."

Elise had heard the name before. Only once, and spoken by her father.

"Old Bonecrack is a dangerous beast who lives in the evening woods," said the messenger. "Lately he's been emerging on the far side of the woods, killing and injuring a great many people." He leaned towards her and smiled a small, patronizing smile. As if she were still a child, and not thirteen years old. She had delivered a calf just this past spring, and could snap a chicken's neck with no trouble. "Now, isn't that sad?" he asked. "And wouldn't it be wonderful if your mother could help us stop him?"

His voice was smooth as honey, and sickly-sweet. The sound of it revolted her. A growl rose unbidden from the pit of her stomach, but she clamped it down, and said, "Yes, I suppose it would, sir." Mother always told her not to upset the messengers.

The voices outside had fallen quiet. Mother returned, and Elise knew that she had won by the sour look on Grandmother's face.

"I accept your offer," she said.

The messenger stood fluidly, like water rising from a pond after a pebble had been dropped in its depths. "You are doing a great service to the duke, and to your king," he said, smiling. His teeth were moon-white.

Mother said nothing more as she signed the commission. No bargaining, because there was nothing more to bargain for.

She helped Mother with her gear, fetching the hunting boots, strapping on the padded leather tunic and helping her into the chain shirt.

"Elise," she said, after her head had emerged from the shirt, which fell rattling down her body and settled into place. She lowered herself to one knee and took her by the shoulders, so close that Elise could smell the lavender her mother used to perfume her hair. She took a deep breath. "If we could send you to school," she said, "a fine school like they have in the capitol, would you go?"

A school in the capitol? She had never considered it. It was as far away as dreaming could be, like asking what she would do if the walls burst open with gold.

"I don't know," she said. "Can't I learn my figures well enough here?"

Her mother laughed. "Elise," she said, "they could teach you so much more than your figures, though! You could learn to be a doctor, if you wanted. You wouldn't have to work in the mills."

Her grandmother had worked at the mills. Her hands were knobby and pained her now, all the time, and the fingers of her ruined right hand barely moved. It was the same with all the women who worked there; the girls in the marketplace talked of it as if it were an inevitable fact of life. They talked of trying to get husbands and become mothers "before their hands went."

She held out her hands and looked at them: the smooth joints, the arch of black dirt beneath her fingernails, the calluses from house chores. She imagined them clean, pressed against flesh, carefully setting bones and stitching wounds closed, finding places where the blood flowed wrong and sending it back the right way.

Her heart bounced unexpectedly. She saw herself tall and clean and polished as a sword, healing not just her own mother but others, too.

"Think about it for me, alright?" Mother brushed a strand of hair out of Elise's eyes. Suddenly she grasped her in both arms, and buried her worn brown face in Elise's hair. Then she took a deep breath, and her shoulders rose and her back straightened as if she were transforming into a different shape altogether, harder and fiercer but still wrapped like armor around her daughter.

"Listen to your grandmother," said Mother. "I will be back in the morning."

Elise nodded. She wanted to say something, but a lump was stuck in her throat. The moment passed, and Mother rose and took her pike.

Grandmother opened the door and let her pass. "Come, my sparrow," she said to Elise, extending her good hand, "let's go see your mother off."

A cold feeling ran through her like a spear: the thrill of seeing her mother's departure at last, and the dawning of what it meant this time. Her father had gone hunting Old Bonecrack. He had taken the evening path, and not returned.

"Mother," said Elise, running out into the night and grabbing her mother's mailed arm. "You don't have to do this, really! I don't need to go to some fancy faraway school. I don't mind. I'll work in the mills. We'll be fine, really!" It all came tumbling out in a rush, and Elise doubted half of what she said was even true. But she didn't want her mother to die.

Mother said nothing, only uncurled Elise's fingers from her arm and smiled. "Be good for me," she said. She put a finger to Elise's lips, a thick and callused finger strong enough to hold back the tide of protests.

Elise felt her grandmother's hands on her shoulders, holding her back. Grandmother's hands, brown and wrinkled and ruined. She watched unblinking as Mother stepped onto the water-bright evening path. The silver light illuminated her, rising along her body until she seemed to be light itself. Then she was a glimmer, and then—gone. Swallowed up into the dark.

The messenger came up beside them, moving through the long grasses with a soft hiss. "Your mother will be fine," he said. "I have the utmost faith in her skill. Now why don't we all go inside before we catch a chill?" His warm-honey voice poured over her, sweet and sticky. The evening path sang to her, and for one hot moment she wanted to rip his throat out. But Grandmother took her hand and led her back to the house, and the bloody dream vanished.

When they were inside and the door shut, the crackling of the hearthfire overwhelmed the faraway song in her skull. Grandmother gave her shoulder a squeeze. "Why don't you go upstairs?"

Elise looked up, but there was no warning in Grandmother's tone, no hard discipline in her face. Only an invitation.

"Yes, Grandmother," she said. Sparing one last glance at the messenger, she climbed the ladder to her bed and quietly unlatched the window. Propping her elbow on the sill and her chin in her hand, she let the night breeze wash over her and fill her lungs. Far below, the evening paths shimmered and sang.

At the edge of the woods, a blackness detached itself from more blackness. Elise straightened, senses alert. Beasts from the evening paths never emerged near their cottage; they were attracted by the glow of towns and villages, the scent of many lives clustered together.

No, it wasn't a beast. It was a man, broad of shoulder and stomach. He was stepping onto one of the evening paths: the same one her mother had taken. The soft light of the path rose and enveloped him, shining on a polished breastplate, and a sword.

He smelled like murder.

Elise scrambled down the ladder. The messenger was spooning dried leaves into the teapot, effusing about the rarity and refinement of sugar rose tea. Grandmother was eyeing the pot with an uncertain frown.

"Grandmother," said Elise, "there's someone else on the path. He just followed Mother."

Grandmother's old eyes narrowed. She opened the door and looked out into the night. "Why would anyone—? No..." She turned to the messenger, her wrinkled face hardening into rage. "It's a trap, isn't it? You—"

Her head tilted back, a flower of blood blooming at her throat. The messenger's hand had moved so quickly, left an arc of silver where the dagger had passed. She collapsed without a sound, as if she were nothing but bones held up by her dress.

The messenger lunged for Elise. Without thinking, she swung the steaming teapot into his face. He staggered backwards, screaming obscenities.

Grandmother blinked, her lifeblood leaking out onto the worn floorboards. She moved her arm slowly, as if she were only half-asleep, and extended one bony, mill-broken finger toward the door.

Toward the evening paths.

Yes, grandmother.

Elise ran out the front door and into the dew-cool meadow. The messenger cried out for her to stop, his legs tearing through the long grass behind her. Her bare feet touched the evening path. A cool tingling ran through the soles of her feet. The meadow and trees and everything she knew didn't vanish as she expected. Instead it flipped: trees became shadows and shadows became trees, and for a single nauseous moment she thought she was running upside down into their twisting labyrinthine branches. The cool sensation beneath her feet turned suddenly sharp and cutting as a winter chill. And then the world righted itself.

She was standing in the evening woods.

She stumbled forward, ready to run. The rush of her own blood filled her ears, and the smell of Grandmother's blood was in her nose. The messenger could not be far behind. She needed to warn Mother.

But the sudden dark of the wood gave way to soft light, and she looked, and her breath caught in her throat.

Her mother had never told her it was beautiful. The trees, twisted and knobby as Grandmother's fingers, glowed with streaks of phosphorescent lichen. Flowers bloomed in their branches, moon-white and sweetly scented. Distant creatures whirred and twittered, making noises that were strange and yet not quite unfamiliar, as if she had heard them in dreams.

A bird landed on a broken tree just off the path; its feathers glowed with that same phosphorescence, the light shifting through its plumage like waves. It looked so similar to the bluejerries that sang in the barn beams that Elise felt her heart calming. It tilted its head and began to sing.

A talon snapped around it. A larger bird landed on the tree, flapping shimmering blue-black wings for balance, and lifted the crushed songbird to its long, scythe-like beak. Its legs were thick and arm-like, too long for its body, and its talons were shaped like hands.

It fixed one glowing eye on Elise.

The tree it perched on twisted suddenly and snapped its branches, and the bird vanished into a mouth that hadn't been there a moment before. A chunk of blue-black feathers drifted softly from the knobby, distended hole.

A scream rose in her throat. She clapped her hand over her mouth and forced it down, choking. A scream would only bring more hunters.

Be still, came a voice from inside her. *Listen.*

She was not sure whose voice it was. Her own thoughts, or the woods singing softly in her head.

She took a deep breath, willing her heart to slow, willing her blood to calm. She listened. Down the path, something heavy stalked through the mud. Its breath was soft and deep. She turned to look.

It was a wolf—or like one in shape. But its teeth were needle-sharp and curved, and so long that it could not close its lips over them. Like it carried a bone cage in its mouth, whose bars were so close-packed that she could not see what it concealed inside.

It paused, and stared at her with eyes like stars. Its nose twitched; it was inhaling her scent, tasting her. She stood still, but could not stop the trembling that shook her from teeth to toes.

It lowered its head and moved on.

Something large and clumsy crashed through the underbrush, making its way towards her. "Little girl, come here!" the messenger cried, his honey voice tight and strained. "You shouldn't be out in the evening woods now. Your grandmother is terribly worried. She's all right, it was just a little accident..."

Branches snapped at his passing, mud squelched beneath his boots. He was so loud.

"Where are you, little girl?" he growled. His voice was rougher now, dirt mixed in his honey. "How can anyone see in this pitch..." he muttered. She saw him clearly now, lit by the glowing trees. He stumbled forward, waving his arms, smacking branches aside as if he were stumbling in utter darkness. "Little girl, where are you? Come out, come—"

He made so much noise. But the thing that killed him did not. A shadow moved across the path, his words cut off into a garbled cry, and then he was gone.

She ran.

The path led her deep into the woods. The smell of blood was everywhere here, and the sound of things killing other things. Bile rose in her throat. She stumbled to a stop, gagging. Her cheeks were wet with tears she hadn't even known she'd been crying. She pressed her hand against her mouth. Where was her mother?

She took a deep breath, pressed her fingertips to her temples. Her senses were even stronger in here than they were back home. She pushed them outward, without strain; like a key fitting into a well-oiled lock, the world opened up. The evening woods glowed as bright as day.

Here was the path her mother's boots had trampled flat for a hundred commissions. Here was the lingering blood-scent of her pursuer, there where heavy boots had bruised the undergrowth. There on that tree was a flock of birds bright as stars, silent and unmoving.

She smelled her mother: a familiar mix of worn leather, sweat, and lavender. She pushed her senses farther out. The sound of Mother's breathing came to her ears, and the steady, firm beat of her heart. She tracked the scent down the path, saw where it opened upon a moonlit glade. Her mother knelt there. Her hands were clasped in her lap, her head was bent. Her pike lay in the long grass at her side, its deadly tip shining softly in the moonlight.

Elise slowed and came to a silent stop, crouching in the shadows between the trees. The dark hulk of the armored man stood like a monolith between them.

He made no noise. He was watching her mother.

Mother hadn't seen them yet. Her eyes were closed, and all her being seemed bent on a pile of rocks in front of her—a crude cairn, Elise realized, meant to conceal the bones of the dead.

Her father's bones. Her father, who had gone hunting Old Bonecrack and had been cracked by him, his life broken open and spilled out onto the grass.

The armored man was going to kill her mother. The thought of it jolted through her body; the trees' soft glow flared, and the night grew even sharper. She saw every detail now, every soft black hair on the man's head, every chink in his armor. His helmet was tucked beneath his arm; the back of his head was open, soft, defenseless.

She knelt in the underbrush and picked up a rock. It was the size of her fist but so much heavier, and sharper, too. Her mother came here to fight monsters, here where everything killed everything else. Why should her daughter be otherwise?

She crept forward.

A rumble ran through the earth. It was a sound like a mountain moving, waking from sleep. She hesitated, listening. The sound grew louder, closer: the stamp of something old and angry upon the earth.

It rose into the glade like a shadow rising to block the moon. Its four legs were thick as old tree trunks. Its heavy, boulderous body, half again as tall as her mother, was armored all over with plates of horny leather. Its craggy head swung low, sniffing the air. A single horn, thick and blunt and curving, rose from the end of its muzzle. The tip was stained dark with old blood. Blue fire shone from its eyes, and between its teeth.

Mother picked up her pike and climbed to her feet. She bowed once to the creature, as if to a sparring partner.

Elise stared. "Old Bonecrack," she said. The name thrummed through her and rang out into the night, as if she were a fiddle string plucked by its presence. Her numb fingers dropped the stone.

Mother and the armored man both turned at the sound of her voice. The man grabbed her by the arms before she could run. A soft cry escaped Mother's lips, a cry of distress Elise had never heard her make before. It frightened her.

Old Bonecrack screamed like rusted iron scraping stone, and began to charge, its thick legs pounding the ground into submission. Mother had to look away from her. She raised her pike, and ran to meet it.

Elise tried to yank herself away from the man, but her weight could not budge him. He merely lifted a finger to his lips. His self-assured smile told her all she needed to know: that she was too late, that there was nothing she could do now to help her mother. And nothing he would do to help her, either.

He pulled her close, held her still, and together they watched.

Old Bonecrack came with a noise like an avalanche, its bloody horn thrusting forward. Mother danced around him, smaller but more nimble, darting in with her pike and darting out again, trying to force the shining fang of it between the plates of its armored hide. Here and there, it caught; here and there, little rivulets of blood welled up. But it was not enough. Old Bonecrack had so much blood, so much life hidden deep inside him. Elise could smell it.

Mother darted into the trees on the other side of the glade. Old Bonecrack stormed after her, but the trees here were old and thick. He could not force his bulk between them. He pushed and heaved and roared, wedging himself in. His trunk-like feet stamped the earth uselessly, his shoulders scraped the trees raw of bark. Her mother, her brilliant and clever mother, charged forward and drove the pike into one gleaming eye.

Old Bonecrack screamed. The pike had not gone in deep enough to kill. The fire in his eye went out, but the fire in his open throat grew to a burning brilliance. With a rumbling lurch, he surged forward, shouldering trees aside.

Mother danced back, drawing her dagger. But there was nowhere to go. The ground behind her dropped away sharply into a ravine. She was cornered.

Elise caught her mother's sudden glance, and knew at once what must happen. Bonecrack would follow her mother relentlessly, and if she led him back away from the cliff, it would only be to bring him closer to Elise. So she did the only thing she could. She slipped over the edge and vanished. Elise screamed. Old Bonecrack, too large to stop his forward progress, disappeared after her, rolling like a boulder down the slope, shattering trees as he went.

It took a long time for the sound to die down. The silence that followed was unbearable.

The armored man pushed Elise aside and dashed off into the woods, following the swath of destruction. Half dreaming, she followed him. She climbed down the slope, clinging to smaller trees still standing along the edge of the splintered path. Her feet found footholds easily, by instinct—as if she had always moved through these woods, as if she remembered them from her dreams. She landed in a small clearing, making no noise.

Old Bonecrack was dying. His neck and back were broken, his spine twisted by his own weight. The fire in his throat flickered like a ghost. Her mother lay pinned beneath one of his trunklike legs, her face ashen and eerie in the moonlight. She did not move to free herself. She was broken, just like him.

She turned her face towards the armored man. "You are the duke?" she said, between long and labored breaths. "It was to be your kill, wasn't it? You, who took its head to the king and claimed the reward?"

The armored man was silent for a moment, regarding Mother as if she, too, were a strange sort of beast he had never seen before. He withdrew a knife, silver-sharp and long as his forearm. "For your service," he said, stepping closer, "I will grant you a mercy."

Elise screamed. She ran from the shadows and threw herself over her mother, snarling up at the armored man. "You will not touch her!"

The duke took a step back, one eyebrow lifting. "Child," he said, "step aside." There was no malice in his voice. It was all so casual, such a minor thing he did, tossing aside the lives of her mother and grandmother, for glory or wealth or honor. His heart beat crimson—she could hear it pounding in her ears—and yet her mother's life was nothing to him, nothing at all.

The forest grew brighter. She saw everything now, smelled it all on the breeze. The blood and sweat of beasts, the scent of crushed flora, the beat and stretch of muscles moving bones, of roots digging deep into soil, of earth grinding on earth. It was all her, she could sense all of it as if it were her own body. And blood, so much blood! Pounding through veins and pouring from wounds and dripping down the throats of those that fed.

Everything here killed everything else. Everything killed without a sound.

She felt the duke now with all her senses: his armor gleaming like a beacon in the soft moonlight, the cold sweat of growing fear sliding down his face and seeping up through his padded layers. In the evening woods, he was so small. Such a tiny life, so easily breakable.

She spoke and the woods heard her, and obeyed. His death was swift: the earth rose up, root and branch snapped shut like a giant hand and dragged him screaming down. He made so much noise. She did not.

She understood now. All of it. Her mother had grown strong on the meat of the creatures who dwelled here, but she had grown up on it. Her body thrummed with the power of the evening woods. She was a part of this place. She killed without a sound.

She could stay here. It would be so easy to stay. She saw herself as she could be: clothed in furs, smeared with blood, her feet as tough as stones. She would have no need for commissions.

A hand closed over hers. The dream-her faded like smoke. Her consciousness shrank down again, pouring back into her small and trembling child-self, still huddled over her broken mother.

Mother stroked her hair with one callused, dirt-encrusted hand. "My Elise...," she whispered, because she had no breath for anything louder. "This is a terrible place to stay."

The last of her self snapped back into place. Her mother's eyes fluttered and closed, like a candle flickering out.

She knelt for a long time in the clearing. Gradually, the sky began to lighten. Soon the paths leading home would fade, and then it would be too late.

But what would she go back home to? Mother and Grandmother were dead, and she was alone. Her mother's pike, that had once been her father's, was shattered and useless; the stump of it was still buried deep in Bonecrack's eye. And even if she used their little savings for a new weapon, no one would commission a young girl to hunt in the evening woods. Only the mills would hire her.

Her eyes fell on the huge bulk of Old Bonecrack, the last thing her mother had won for her. The last monster she slew, in the hope that Elise could do something better. A bird alighted on its thick, bumpy head, iridescent feathers faintly gleaming. It began to sing a morning song.

Squinting, she could see the shadows of other trees behind the dark, twisted trees of this place. Day trees, straight-trunked and familiar.

She did not realize until she saw them how much she missed those trees. Standing straight among their straight, tall trunks, she saw the other self she had imagined, the other future: a doctor clean and bright as a blade.

She pulled the duke's sword from its scabbard and held it against Old Bonecrack's thick neck. It would have taken time if she had been her old self, but now it took only a moment, a burst of power from the evening woods, to bring the sword up and down again and cut the head clean off. Another flick of power, and the earth opened and gently pulled her mother down into itself. A third command, a whisper, brought a tussock of grass at her feet into bloom, and then to seed. She plucked the thick-grained stems and tucked them inside her sleeve. Then she hefted Old Bonecrack's head, and walked from the woods via the first fading silver strand she found.

The messenger's tall, heart-hollow horse still waited in the barn. The grains she had brought with her tingled with the power of the evening woods; they would heal the hole in his heart. She would give him a good life, and he would carry her far away to the king. She would go to school and learn to be a proper doctor. The power of the evening woods was in her blood, and in her hands. She would heal many.

The rising sun made her eyes water. Behind her, the evening woods disappeared.

Jennifer Hykes lives with her husband and two cats just outside of Pittsburgh, PA. She can frequently be found with a cup of tea in hand. She has often felt the pull of strange paths, and enjoys telling stories in order to find out where they go. Her work has previously appeared in Betwixt, Abyss & Apex, PodCastle, and Apex Magazine.

AFTERWORD

It's always hard to put something down and walk away. I left the Triangulation staff once before, then came back when I had the chance to make the book my own. I'm proud of what we accomplished, this year and last. Working on an anthology is a unique combination of love and frustration, and I know that I'll miss being a part of it. But it's time for me to step aside and let someone else take the reins.

Triangulation will always be important to me, just like every story I've ever written shapes the next. Things have changed so much since I started— the first year that I read stories, we actually met in person, every week, to read and talk about the submissions. Now, I have people on my staff who haven't even met each other. The current process is much more streamlined, more efficient, more convenient. But I have to admit, I miss reading out really amazing (or really terrible) passages of the pieces we're looking at to each other, and having instant feedback from another human's face instead of just their words on a screen. The pizza was nice, too.

I wouldn't have made it here without the editors who worked on Triangulation in the past—Diane Turnshek, Barbara Carlson, Pete Butler, Bill Moran, and Steve Ramey—and the people who helped me this year— Kathryn Board, Jon Carroll Thomas, Douglas Gwilym, Frank Oreto, Laine Wooliscroft, and Barbara Carlson (who is a treasure, and the real force behind this anthology coming out every year). I also have to thank my husband, Paul Stefko, for being awesome and helping out so much more than I should have asked him to.

Thank you for picking up *Triangulation: Beneath the Surface*. I hope you enjoy the stories as much as I enjoyed picking them out for you.

And now, this is the part where I drop the mic.

~Jamie Lackey, 2016

STAFF BIOS

Kathryn Board has published short stories in the fantasy, sci-fi, and horror genres. She has also published a book of erotic fiction. When she isn't writing, she plays repetitive but addictive games on her phone, argues politics on-line with strangers, and analyzes the effectiveness of television commercials. Kathryn lives in Pennsylvania with her very patient partner of fifteen years.

Barbara Carlson lives in Pittsburgh with her husband, cat and 25 ferrets (she runs a ferret shelter). She helped organize Parsec many years ago with Ann Cecil, and has been involved with science fiction fandom since 1980. She runs registration for Confluence, manages the Parsec and Confluence websites (among others), assembles the calendar for the WPAM Mensa group, creates the ferret club newsletter and does the occasional editing job. In her spare time, she enjoys making polymer clay aliens.

Douglas Gwilym is a writer and a talker (hopefully in that order). He's ravenous for family stories and weird local history. His handlebar mustache sings and plays bass for sick rock bands. He stands up and reads his stories of darkness and heart whenever the humans allow. His novels are about giants, mystic plumbers, and magical math-genius punk rock grrlz.

Benjamin Hitmar lives in Pittsburgh developing concepts and designs for various groups in the entertainment industry. Compared to that work, painting is a way to create in a more primal frame of mind.

Jamie Lackey lives in Pittsburgh with her husband and their cat. She has over 120 short fiction credits, and has appeared in *Daily Science Fiction*,

160

Beneath Ceaseless Skies, and the Stoker Award-winning *After Death....* She's a member of the Science Fiction and Fantasy Writers of America. Her short story collection, *One Revolution*, and her science fiction novella, *Moving Forward*, are available on Amazon.com. Her debut novel, *Left-Hand Gods*, will be available from Hadley Rille Books in July 2016. In addition to writing, she spends her time reading, playing tabletop RPGs, baking, and hiking. You can find her online at www.jamielackey.com.

Frank Oreto was raised by radical leftist Italian carnie barkers with predictable results. In between secret missions, he writes, edits, and raises children in Pittsburgh, PA. Sometimes his beard changes color.

Jon Carroll Thomas is currently best described as a stay-at-home dad that that sometimes writes, edits, and reviews weird fiction. He lives in Raleigh, North Carolina with his wife, son, and cats.

Laine Wooliscroft is a podcaster, filmmaker, and writer who dreams of a world where all media is creatively content-driven, coffee is bottomless, and you can bring your cat to work every day.

As a story-teller with over 12 years of experience, she is a co-host of the podcast "Super Serials," which is quickly approaching 10,000 downloads, and her documentary film, "Nip, Tuck, Click," has been presented several times in the state this year by the National Organization for Women.

When she's not re-reading Sweet Valley High books or writing short stories, Laine can be found attempting yoga, pawing through an estate sale, and cooking meals at home with good friends.

"Super Serials," is available for free on iTunes and Stitcher.

www.ingramcontent.com/pod-product-compliance
Lightning Source LLC
Chambersburg PA
CBHW031113260626
47172CB00001B/343